The Duke of Ravens

Regency Hearts

Book 3

Jennifer Monroe

Copyright © 2019 Jennifer Monroe

All rights reserved.

This book is a work of fiction. Names, characters, businesses, places, events and incidents are either the products of the author's imagination or used in a fictitious manner. Any resemblance to actual persons, living or dead, or actual events is purely coincidental.

Regency Hearts Series

The Duke of Fire

Return of the Duke

The Duke of Ravens

Duke of Storms

Chapter One

The crackling of the wood in the fireplace was deafened by the conversation of those attending the party at Blackwood Estates. Caroline Hayward, Duchess of Browning, smiled politely as a couple, whose name she could not recall, walked toward her, laughing at some private joke. They stopped long enough to return her smile with one of their own, presumably genuine, before moving past her toward the table that held various cakes and finger foods.

She followed them with her eyes, her thoughts filled with wonder. She had often dreamed of possessing joyfulness like those around her, and by all outward appearances, she should be happy. Married to her husband of five years, she now owned the finest of dresses and gowns, expensive jewelry, and had more servants than she would ever need.

So, why was she not happy? Perhaps it was the fact she had no one in which to confide. So many secrets hid away inside her, words she wished to utter, to let someone know of her pain. Yet she could not do such a thing and knew she never would. Not because she lacked the courage to do so, but rather she was afraid of the repercussions that would follow. She was unsure what she feared more; the rumors that were likely to make their rounds or the swift hand of her husband.

Reginald was quick to anger, and over the last five years, Caroline had learned to adhere to the old adage that women should be seen and not heard.

Or was that children? she wondered. It mattered not, for the saying applied to her regardless.

Smiling at another couple, she raised her wine glass and took a polite sip as she looked over the ornate ballroom. In the far corner played a string quartet, the violin melody threatening to lift her off her feet. Guests were laughing and drinking, clearly pleased with the party. That gratified her; it was the point of these functions, was it not?

Her eyes fell on her husband across the room, and she frowned. He was engaged in conversation with a woman, Miss Mary French, whose morals were as loose as the tongue of a drunken lout. Watching the two, Caroline felt her heart drop, for she knew all too well that what the duke wanted, he would get. And judging by his lustful expression, he wanted that woman.

Letting out a sigh, Caroline took another sip of her wine, pushing out her frustrations about Reginald. Nothing she could say or do would change the man, so why waste time on such worries? Instead, she turned her thoughts to their son, Oliver. The boy had just turned five and was the only light in her otherwise dark world. The time she spent with him she cherished, whether it was reading him a story or allowing the boy to use his exceptional imagination to tell one of his own.

"Duchess," a female voice said.

Caroline turned and smiled at the older woman she knew well. "Lady Barnsfield," she said as she leaned down to give the tiny baroness a kiss on the cheek, "are you enjoying the party?"

"I most certainly am," the woman said, her voice a raspy breath. "In fact, I was just telling Harold how your parties are always my favorite. And I must say," she said as she gave an appreciative smile, "you look absolutely beautiful in that gown." Lady Barnsfield had always been a kindly soul, and Caroline appreciated the fact the woman had always treated her as a daughter. In most cases, others of the peerage wished only to use her as a means to get to her husband, but not Lady Barnsfield. When she spoke, it was with honesty, and few people appreciated it more than Caroline. More than likely because she did not always have kind words for everyone.

"I am glad you are enjoying yourself," Caroline said, honest for the first time that night. "And, as for the gown, I do like it." She glanced down at the rich blue velvet trimmed with white lace. The neckline emphasized her bosom much more than she would have liked, but Reginald had insisted—no, he ordered—she purchase it the week prior. It would not have been Caroline's first choice, but she did what she was told and that was that.

She and Lady Barnsfield continued with their pleasantries, and the conversation turned to Lord Barnsfield and his pitiful snoring. The poor woman was clearly starved for company, much like Caroline herself.

"Oh, there he goes again drinking another brandy," Lady Barnsfield said, her eyes narrowing. "More than two and his snores will wake the entire household. Forgive me for leaving, but I must go and stop him."

Caroline giggled as the woman walked away. Despite the complaints the baroness gave, she had made it perfectly clear how much love she had for her husband.

If only I could be as fortunate, she thought.

She finished the remainder of her wine and set the empty glass on a side table for one of the servants to retrieve. Even after five years, leaving to others that which needed to be done felt odd, but what else could she do? If the people had no work, they would have no reason to be employed, thus losing their positions and being without an income. Without an income, people would have no means on which to live, and Caroline could not see that happen to even one of the servants.

Another glass was thrust into her hand before she knew what was happening, and she turned to face a man who resembled Reginald in so many ways, he could have been his twin despite the difference of twelve years in age. Neil Hayward was nearing fifty, but he had the same deep lines in his face and gray hair on his head as Reginald, making both appear closer to seventy.

"I thought you could use another," Neil said with an air of self-assurance.

Caroline bent her head slightly. "Thank you." She made a purposeful glance around the room. "Everyone seems happy, do they not?"

The man gave a nod of agreement, but his eyes remained on her breasts. His ogling made her sick; the only thing lacking in his gaze was drool dripping from the corner of his mouth.

She stared at the man, finding it difficult to hide her repulsion—he was the brother of her husband, after all. If he had been any other man and she any other woman, even one titled as she was, arguments would arise. Yet her husband cared not for how she was treated by anyone, especially his brother.

"Indeed," Neil replied to her question. "Many are enjoying themselves immensely, but some are growing bored like me. Perhaps you can show me to a guest room."

His eyebrows rose, and Caroline thought her stomach would empty on the spot. She had no trust for this man, and she certainly would not walk anywhere alone with him, but most especially to a room with a bed.

She attempted to temper the panic that tried to rise in her as she glanced around the room to find any excuse to deny him. When her gaze returned to him, his smile had widened, the lust behind his eyes clear.

"Would you not like to remain and keep me company for a few moments?" she asked with a smile she could barely form. "I am sure we could alleviate your boredom by joining another group in conversation."

His crooked smile did nothing to hide the anger that flashed in his eyes. "Of course, that would be a delight." He glanced away. "Oh, one moment please."

He walked over to speak with a man around her own age of four and twenty. A few moments later, both men returned.

"Duchess Hayward, may I introduce Lord Christopher Grandstone, Marquess of Trapton."

Lord Grandstone gave her a polite bow. "Your Grace."

Caroline nodded her acknowledgment. The man seemed pleasant enough, and Caroline welcomed the distraction for Neil.

"Grandstone has just graduated from University," Neil said, "and will be returning to Oxford to lecture on government something or other in Africa."

Mr. Grandstone shook his head. "Actually, I will be speaking of the abysmal treatment of orphans in Africa, but I would not wish to bore you with the details."

"Not at all," Caroline replied. Any topic had to be better than anything Neil had to say. Plus, she did find herself interested in the subject matter, even if she knew virtually nothing about Africa or its orphans.

She breathed a sigh of relief when Neil walked away, and she relaxed. The man made her feel as if her gown had been infested with bedbugs.

"Orphans in Africa?" she said with interest now that Neil was gone. "What made you decide to speak on such a subject?"

"I hope to educate a new generation of men about the atrocities that are happening on that continent, especially in…"

As he continued to speak, something from the corner of Caroline's eye caught her attention. Neil had gone to her husband and was now pointing a finger in her direction.

Reginald frowned, and panic washed over Caroline.

"I'm sorry," she said, interrupting the man mid-sentence, "but I must see to something."

"Oh, well, if you must…"

Before she could get away, her husband's cold hand was on her arm, his fingers digging into the flesh. She knew better than to react, even if his grasp pained her, for all too many times she had been forced to remain in her rooms for a minimum of three days so no one would see the bruises he had left in the wake of his anger.

"Pardon me," Reginald said with a curt tone, though he did not look at Mr. Grandstone. "I must speak to my wife for a moment." He did not release his grasp as he led her from the room.

The sounds of laughter and music faded as he led her up the stairs. At the top, he grabbed a single candle from one of the stands, cursing when the hot wax dripped on his fingers.

"Reginald, you are hurting me," Caroline said now that they were alone. She did not struggle; that would bring on even more pain.

"You have angered me once again," he growled as he led her to a far door. He removed a key from his vest pocket and inserted it into the lock before pulling the door open.

"What have I done?" she asked, trying to keep her fear at bay but failing miserably.

Her jaw cracked as his fist made contact with it, and tiny pinpricks played in her vision. "Thrusting your body toward any man who looks your way?" he said, stepping in close to her, his breath hot on her face. "You are an embarrassment and a harlot. I should throw you back to the streets where I found you!"

Tears streamed down her cheeks as she rubbed her chin. That would leave a purpling that would last much longer than three days.

"You are to remain here tonight. Do not leave. Tomorrow I will decide on your punishment, but for now, I will enjoy the remainder of my evening. But worry not, for I will not be alone. At least there are those who know how to show me the respect I deserve."

He pushed her through the door, the weak light of the candle lighting up a small room with a tiny window that contained only a small bed as the only form of furnishings. There was no commode, only a simple bucket where she could relieve herself.

"Oliver," she whispered. "May I at least kiss our son goodnight?"

He snorted. "No. The boy is weak enough already. He does not need you fawning over him any longer. That will be the next thing we will improve; the way you coddle the boy. But I do not wish to discuss it now. I have more entertaining matters to attend to." He let out a cough as he closed the door, leaving her in darkness, and locked the door behind him.

Caroline sobbed as she crawled across the unfinished wooden floor and felt around for the low bed. On it, she curled up into a ball and wept.

As her ears adjusted to the silence of the room, she could just make out the muffled noises of the party below. Her husband would make excuses for her, and the guests would accept them without a single thought for her.

She stood and walked over to the window. No moon or stars winked in the sky. Just as her life, it had been cast in darkness.

Chapter Two

Caroline put all her weight into the hoe one last time and the dirt broke. Finally. She had been working on the tiny garden outside her family home all afternoon, but the drought had made working even this tiny plot difficult. There would be no harvest this year, and her father raved inside the house, the last of their money spent on spirits.

The sound of a horse approaching made Caroline turn, and a faceless man rose up, his roan lifting its hooves regally, as if proud to carry the man who sat upon his back.

"You, girl," the man called out, "I would speak to your father."

Before she could respond, her father stumbled out the door. "Ah, Your Grace, you came!"

"Of course I came," the man said with a snort. "I said I would, did I not?"

Her father rubbed his chin. "I suppose you did at that. Please, come in."

The man looked at her expectantly and she rushed up to grab the reins as he dismounted. He gave her an appraising glance up and down, and Caroline could not help but shiver. She had a bad feeling about this.

She stood there, holding the reins of the horse as if she had nothing better to do. Inside, voices muffled by the closed door, her father and the man talked. Then the door flew open, and her father walked out, wearing a smile large enough to split his face in two.

"We are saved!" he shouted.

Caroline looked at him with shock. "We are? Did this man bring rain?"

Her father gave her a stern look. "Of course, not, child. He is paying off all our debt, and we will own the deed to the land. Just think! I will own my own house and land!"

Suspicion crept into Caroline's mind. "In exchange for what?" she asked.

The unknown man then stepped from the door. "For your hand in marriage, of course," he said. Then his facial features came into focus, allowing Caroline to recognize him, and she screamed.

Caroline woke with a start, her heart pounding in her chest. She had not dreamed of the day her father had traded her for the small cottage and the land on which it sat, not since the last time Reginald had locked her in the room. The fact she had experienced the dream before did not take away the horror of it.

The first rays of the sun shone through the window onto the bed, providing a little warmth, though she felt cold inside. She had cried herself to sleep, worried about her son. Reginald had not returned once he locked the door, not that she had expected him to, of course. Many nights she had dreamed of leaving Blackwood Estates, taking Oliver with her. The two would escape into the night and find residence elsewhere, and maybe she would find someone to love her.

Those dreams did not come last night. Perhaps it was evil of her to imagine another man in her life, for she was a married woman. Granted she was treated with contempt, but perhaps that was the expected life of a duchess. Her father had never struck her mother at any point in Caroline's upbringing, but perhaps her mother was as good at hiding such horror from her daughter as Caroline was at hiding it from her son.

She looked down at her wrinkled gown. Margaret would have a difficult time ironing out the creases in the material, but the woman never made a complaint. If anything, she looked upon Caroline with sadness. Not pity, thankfully, but at least she did feel sorry for Caroline, although they never discussed what both knew was the truth of her marriage—her husband was a tyrant.

She shivered as she thought of her wedding night. It had been nothing as she had imagined. He had demanded she remove her clothing, and he flung her on the bed and went about his duty as a duke—and as her husband. Their intimacy was anything but intimate, and when he was finished, he left her alone in the bed.

Later, finding out she was with child, he had merely sniffed, but he continued to have his way with her whenever he felt the urge, until the doctor had informed him it would be unsafe to the baby she carried. Reginald had not been happy at the prospect of not having his desires satiated, thus he went in search of other means in which to do so. And although she had tried to appease him over the years, her smiles were never returned and her attempts at affection were rebuked.

The one relief she had was a set of her own rooms, a sanctuary of sorts. A smaller room had been set up for Oliver, but as soon as he was what the duke deemed of an appropriate age—that being two years—the boy was moved to his own room. It was as if her son had been torn from her, but she hid her sorrow and visited him as often as the nanny would allow.

If that could have been the worst of her time in Blackwood Estates, she would have been relatively happy. Many nights had been spent in the room where she was now. For what reason depended on the duke's mood. If Caroline did not smile at a man, Reginald would grow angry, accusing her of being rude and unsociable. If she did smile, and Reginald was in one of his tempers, he would accuse her of horrible things. The problem was knowing which rule to use in which situation, for his judgment of her would vary from one time to the next.

At other times, he would comment that she disgusted him. This latter was his favorite topic of conversation when they had no guests to stay his tongue. It was the reason she enjoyed when they hosted various functions, for then he typically kept his comments about what he thought of her to himself.

Coming of age in her small village, the looks of men—both married and not—convinced her that she was at least attractive. Her dark hair and blue eyes caused more than one girl to despise her, although she never did anything to bring about their hatred. Perhaps she should have advocated for herself more, but she had not liked being disagreeable to anyone.

The sound of footsteps made her sit up and wrap her arms around her bent knees. She trembled with fear as the key turned in the lock, and when the door opened, Reginald entered, his hand covering his mouth as he coughed. A lingering illness, or so he had said, that he was unable to shake.

"Reginald," Caroline said as she stood, "I would like to apologize." She could not bear another strike of his hand or the lashing of his tongue. Whatever she could do to appease him, she would.

"Remove your clothes," he commanded.

She did as he asked, and as she worked the tiny buttons that ran down her back, she feared he would grow angry once again because she moved too slowly. He did not. Instead, he studied a piece of brown cloth that he had carried in draped over his arm, a sinister grin on his face.

When she finally removed the gown, she stood shivering before him in her shift.

"The shift, as well."

She opened her eyes widely but did as he bade. Was he planning on performing his husbandly duties on her after so long? The thought of that made her sick, and soon she stood before him, bereft of clothing, her arms wrapped around herself to not only keep her warm but to hide her shame.

"Put that on," he said, tossing her the cloth. It was a plain dress made of burlap. She had not owned anything so poor even when she was a child.

When she finished donning the dress, he grabbed her arm and pulled her out into the hallway to stand in front of a small mirror that hung on the wall. "Do you know what I see?"

"No," she whispered. She attempted not to wince at the hold he had on her arm, the bruises left the night before still tender.

"A woman of low class who has been given the opportunity to be a Lady," he said with a sneer. "It seems as though she does not appreciate what she has been given, so today, you will work as the peasant woman you are!"

"Reginald," she begged, "I can explain about last evening." She continued to plead with him as he marched her down the hallway.

He said nothing, but as they passed his bedroom, what was left of any hope Caroline had disappeared. For standing there was Miss Mary French, her long red hair flowing down her back and devoid of any clothing. In her hands was a large necklace of glistening jewels, larger than anything Caroline had ever received.

Hot tears burned down her cheeks as she was led outside. At least the servants had the decency to turn away as she and Reginald walked past, but no one dared intervene. Work was difficult to come by for many these days, so no one was willing to set in to give aid, for they knew the only outcome would be dismissal, and she did not blame them for their hesitancy.

They came to a stop in front of a large sectioned-off square of dirt, and Reginald released her arm. "I want this soil turned by sundown, or you will remain in that room all week."

She nodded as she wiped the tears from her face. How ironic that she would be working a small plot of land even after she married one of the most influential men in the area.

"I understand," she replied. Then she glanced around. "Where are the tools?"

He snorted. "You will use your fingers. I suggest you get started now; time is slipping by."

Caroline looked over the area with concern. "All of it? With my hands?" she asked, shocked that he would make such a demand of her.

"All of it."

Her humiliation deepened when she went to her knees just as Philip, the family's gardener, came around one of the far hedges and stopped to stare.

"Hurry, now," Reginald said. "You are no longer a Lady. You will return to your roots and conduct yourself in the way of your parents."

The words hurt more than ever. Her father had died three years earlier, her mother not two months ago, and she had not been allowed to attend either of their funeral services. For her, that had been worse than the beatings, worse than being locked in that room, and he knew it.

She glanced down at the ill-fitting dress and gasped. "This dress is much too revealing!" she said in a hushed tone. The truth was, if she was not careful and she bent over too far, her bosom would fall right out! Was he devising another reason to be angry with her?

"I assumed you enjoyed the admiration of men," Reginald said in his haughty tone. "You, gardener!" he called out. "Come here."

The man hurried over, his long, dark locks concealing most of his face. Caroline had not realized it before, but she did not remember ever seeing his face, at least not all of it. He always kept his hair so that it came to just below his shoulders, but rather than pull it back as was the fashion, he allowed it to hide his features.

"Your Grace," Philip said with a bow.

"See to it that my wife remains here all day working. I do not want her to rest, nor should she eat or drink. I have business to conduct in town and need someone to keep an eye on her."

"Of course, Your Grace," the man replied with another deep bow. "I will not falter to uphold your command."

The duke gave the man a sniff and then turned and marched away.

With tears running down her face, tears she could not dam, she leaned over and began to claw at the hard soil, pain shooting up her arm as a fingernail caught on a pebble and attempted to pull away.

She worked without stopping, and a short time later, she looked up at the window and pursed her lips. Miss French stood looking out the window as the duke came up behind her. He kissed her neck and then led her away. Although his affairs had been known to her for so long, having the adulterous woman mock her caused a new feeling to come over Caroline.

So, the man had not gone into town yet, more than likely needing to satisfy his cravings beforehand. At least it was not Caroline who had to see to that, for the idea made her ill. After five years of torment, sadness, and shame, a realization came over her as she dug her fingers into the hard soil.

For the first time in years, she was no longer scared. No, her fear was now overtaken by anger.

Chapter Three

Philip Butler stood at attention, his heart going out to the young woman left in his care. At the age of four and thirty, he had seen horrible things in his life. This had to be among the worst he had encountered. No woman should be treated in such a disgraceful manner, regardless of her station in life. Even women of the lower class were not treated as work animals in the manner the duke demanded of his wife.

Employed by Reginald Hayward for four months, Philip was thankful for the work and the wages it paid. In that short time, he had seen what the duke had done to the innocent beauty now on her hands and knees digging in the soil.

It was well-known that the duke was unfaithful to his wife, for he flaunted his mistresses, adorning them with fine clothes and jewelry. Too often, Philip had stumbled across the man performing acts that were meant for private and shared by man and wife.

Yet, this was not the only reason Philip despised the man. He had heard the manner in which the duke spoke to his wife, the sharp tongue he used with her was sickening, and he had witnessed the duke strike her twice. The second time it had happened, Philip had bit on his lip so hard to keep himself from screaming at the man that he drew blood. According to the house servants, the beatings were a common occurrence, and knowing this only fueled the disgust Philip had for him.

A woman of such beauty should be held in high regard, or so he thought. And the duchess was truly unique. Her face seemed sculpted by the finest artist; her eyes sparkled with a light that could have filled a dark night. Her body was shapely, especially in the dress she currently wore; although he refused to stare. Such a beauty did not deserve to be scrutinized with lust but only with respect.

The duchess stopped digging and straightened her back as she wiped sweat from her brow, leaving a streak of dirt across her forehead.

He reached into his pocket and produced a kerchief. "Please," he offered.

She narrowed her eyes at him and then glanced toward the house. "I must refuse," she said in a low tone. "His anger..." Her words trailed off, but she did not need to say them aloud for him to know what she meant.

A sound came to his ear. "Listen."

She glanced around, confusion written on her features. "I hear nothing..."

He held up a single finger to silence her and quickly walked away, moving along the side of the house. Pushing through the shrubbery, he peeked between two branches. His ears had not deceived him. A trail of long red hair disappeared into a waiting carriage followed by the duke. Within a few moments, the carriage pulled away and disappeared down the drive.

"May you never return," Philip whispered after the pair, and then he turned and headed back to where the duchess was back at her tilling.

"Here, drink and cool yourself," he said, handing her a leather pouch that hung from his boxcloth braces where they were attached to the front of his pants. It only held a small amount of water, but it was enough to quench his thirst when he did not wish to stop and ladle water from the barrel behind the shed.

The woman's eyes widened with fear. "I cannot disobey my husband," she said in a shaky voice.

"He is gone," Philip replied, motioning the pouch toward her once again. "Of course, I cannot report what I do not see."

He set the water on a rock beside her and turned as if looking off toward the shed. "It is such a lovely day. I don't suppose rain will be coming judging by those clouds."

He could hear her drinking from the pouch, and he smiled to himself. He pretended to study the sky for several more moments before hearing a quiet "Thank you". Then he turned around to find the pouch back in its place on the rock.

"Do you enjoy working here?" the duchess asked.

He looked down at her lovely features, and he could not stop the thoughts that tore through his mind. They were not the villainous thoughts of rakes and degenerates, but rather of a man whose heart was filled with warmth. Somehow, he found himself wishing that one day the duke would leave her, and she would be available to find a man fitting her elegance and beauty. "Yes, Your Grace, I do," he said in response to her question.

She gave a small smile and squinted as she looked up at him. "There is no reason for formalities here," she said with a sigh. "Please, call me Caroline. I am a peasant, after all." He thought he saw a flare of anger behind her eyes, but it was gone so quickly, he was unsure it had been there.

"Of course," Philip replied, though he was unsure what he thought of her request. Would he be able to see her as a woman and not a duchess? He studied her again and found his answer. Yes, he most certainly could.

"My husband must think highly of you to charge you with the task of watching over me. Though, I do wonder, why did you offer me water when he forbade it? I could tell him you defied him if I chose to do so."

Philip let out a small sigh. "That you could; although, I believe you would not do so."

She raised an eyebrow. "Oh? And why is that?"

"Because I see a woman nobler than the title she carries," he replied. He cursed himself silently. He had a job to do, which was not complimenting the woman before him. "I am sorry for speaking in such a bold manner."

She offered him another of her wonderful smiles, one that was warmer than the sun that heated his back. "Thank you for your words, Philip. They are more comforting than you realize."

He said nothing, for he feared what he might say. Instead, he gave her a nod, and she turned to resume her work. He wanted to kneel at her side and help her with the task she had been given, but he knew he could not. Not only for the fear of the duke learning he had done so, but also because he recognized that she needed the work to aid in venting her anger. No, he had no business taking away from her that which would allow her to become stronger, for she tore at the soil with a vengeance. What she needed was to be left alone.

***

Although he took a great risk, Philip managed to secure some food and more water for Caroline. The woman had gobbled down the food as a street urchin who had not eaten in weeks, her eyes darting fearfully toward the house.

"My ears never fail me," he assured her. "I will hear when he returns."

She gave him a nod and slowed her eating, for which Philip was glad. He could not have her choking on the bread when she was not to be receiving any food whatsoever. She took another drink from the pouch and then handed it to him.

"Thank you," she repeated for the fifth time. "One day I shall repay your kindness for the deeds you have done here today."

He went to tell her that it was not needed, that the payment he sought would not come from her, but a sound caught his attention. He followed her gaze to the back door where her son, Oliver, walked through with his governess. When he turned back to Caroline, the look of longing she had on her face was heart-wrenching. He knew the son was used against her, oftentimes being withheld from her for many days when the duke was angry with her.

"Mother!" the boy cried as he broke free from the grasp of the governess and ran toward Caroline. He was soon in his mother's arms as she planted kisses all over his cheeks.

"Oh, Oliver!" she said as she pushed him away lightly and looked him up and down. "How are your studies?"

The boy hugged her again, and she closed her eyes as if savoring the moment. "I am learning my letters," Oliver said as he pulled away from his mother's grasp. "Miss Lindston says I'm very bright." He paused as he noticed Philip. "Oh, hello."

"Hello, young master," Philip replied with a bow.

Miss Lindston approached, her face filled with concern.

"Is everything all right?" Philip asked the governess as he forestalled her. "You look very upset." Behind him, he could hear Caroline and Oliver talking, Caroline telling her son of her love for him. It was Philip's hope to give them as much time as he could.

"Quite well, Mr. Butler," the governess replied curtly. "His Grace told me…" She paused to lower her voice and lean in. "Not to allow Oliver near his mother today. I must not disobey him."

"I could not agree more," Philip replied. "For to disobey his word would be most unfitting." His mind churned as he thought of a way to keep the woman at bay for longer. "It reminds me of a story my uncle once told me." He tapped his chin. "Wait, perhaps it was my father."

Miss Lindston attempted to look past him, but he shifted in the same direction. "Well, it makes no difference who told me, does it?" He laughed and was amused when the governess gave a distracted laugh. "Well, it was the story of a duke and a servant named David." He paused again. "Wait, do you know this story already by chance?"

"Hardly," Miss Lindston said with a sniff. "Now, pardon me." She pushed past him, and a moment later she grabbed the boy by the hand and pulled him away from Caroline. "Now, Oliver, we must keep to our schedule. Come, it is time for our walk."

Oliver stared at his mother with sadness in his eyes, but he did as the governess asked.

Caroline watched the pair walk away, her eyes clouded with tears. "Once again you have intervened and helped me," she said without looking at him. "I promise I will repay the gesture now twice over. Do not hesitate to tell me what you want when the day comes when I am able to oblige."

"Thank you…Caroline." He would never take that repayment. He had helped the woman, for she was good and not for any form of personal gain. For a brief moment, as he looked at her, he thought that maybe he could love such a woman again. He had experienced that type of love before, and the pain was still much too strong to even consider it risking such a relationship again. Plus, this woman was not available to love; she was a married woman, married to the man who was his employer.

Therefore, with a smile, she turned to continue with her work, and Philip returned to his. He was certain both hoped the duke would be in a better mood upon his return than that in which he had left.

***

The sun was nearing its resting place on the horizon when the duke returned, his mistress at his side. Philip stood straight, his head bowed so his dark hair hung over his face lest his own eyes betray the anger he held. Although he did not mind the time he spent with the duchess, he could not condone such abhorrent behavior from any man, be he duke or peasant. Voicing his opinion would get him dismissed, and this position was much too important to him. This, of course, brought on a bout of guilt for putting his work before the needs of the young woman who was bent over in the dirt, but his dismissal would not help her either, for his words would do nothing to change the course of action the duke had set.

"I see my request has been completed," the duke said.

Caroline went to stand, but the man's hand rested on her shoulder to keep her on her knees.

"Do not rise until I instruct you to do so."

The nod Caroline gave reminded Philip of a child being reprimanded, and in a way, that was the duke's intentions at the moment.

"I hope the lesson you had today has taught you what I expect from you, although you do not seem to learn, for I must teach you daily." He let out a sigh as if he was exasperated, and the woman beside him giggled as she brushed back her red hair.

Philip hid his glare for the woman—Miss French if he had heard correctly. He knew little about clothing for women, but the dress she wore was expertly made and the jewels she wore around her neck were large. She repositioned the pendant that had moved on her bosom when she laughed, clearly wishing to bring attention to both herself and the necklace.

"I apologize for my behavior, Your Grace," Caroline replied meekly. "May I dine with you tonight?"

The man snorted and looked her up and down. "No, I do not wish one of your class dining with me, especially in clothing such as what you wear currently. There is no time for you to ready yourself anyway. Why, by the time the servants heated water…"

"And Oliver? Will he…?"

Philip had been holding his breath. The woman had courage, he had to admit that! Not only to ask another question but to interrupt the duke, as well? Hidden courage indeed.

The duke did not seem to take notice of the slight. "My son will be dining with Miss French and myself. I will have your meal brought out here. That will give the servants time to heat enough water for your bath." He assessed her again, a grimace on his face. "I am afraid you will need twice as much water to wash off all the grime from your body."

Caroline clenched a fist, and Philip worried the woman had been driven to the brink. Would she unleash her fury and jeopardize everything? "But…"

"Your Grace," Philip said before the woman could say anything more—a little too loudly by the manner in which the duke and Miss French jumped, "shall I continue my work here, or may I work elsewhere?"

As he had hoped, the duke redirected his anger from Caroline to Philip—and stopped Caroline from making her situation worse. "Of course, you bumbling fool. You must keep an eye on her." He heaved his arms in the air. "What is it with people around here not listening to me? The sun is not yet set, and I have not dismissed you, so the task I have assigned you has yet to be completed. When she is finished for the night, you may retire.

You should be thankful that I am not docking your pay for your stupidity."

"Yes, Your Grace," Philip said with forced humility. "Thank you for your mercy." He dipped his head further to add to the charade.

The odious man snorted again, and Miss French laughed outright.

Between the curtain of his hair, Philip watched as the two disappeared into the house. He unclenched his jaw and turned to cast his eyes on Caroline.

The woman no longer adorned herself with the humble stance she had in the presence of the duke. Now, she was angry. "You interrupted me!" she said. "What made you believe you could do such a thing? Especially with a woman of my…title." The last word was choked.

"Forgiveness, Your Grace," Philip said with a diffident bow of his head. "I spoke out because I did not wish to see you hurt. At least, not anymore." His voice was now just a whisper.

It became quiet, and Philip remained standing with his hands behind his back. She might be treated as less than who she was by the duke, but Philip had no intentions of doing so himself. He hoped she understood that he had been disrespectful only to ease her suffering.

The butler emerged from the house with a tray that held much less than Philip expected it would have if Caroline had been served in the dining room.

The duchess turned to face Philip, the last light of the evening highlighting her beauty. "Thank you," she whispered before the butler was close enough to hear. "Although, I doubt that anyone can stop my hurt."

Chapter Four

Caroline used the week following her humiliation in the garden to redirect her anger and formulate a plan for her escape. The duke had bestowed enough jewelry and other valuable gifts over the years—not as tokens of affection, of course, but as a means to demonstrate to the *ton* his vast wealth. She could easily sell it all and have adequate funds to sustain both herself and Oliver for several years. It would be her means to set up a new home and allow her time to obtain a position of some sort and build a new life for the two of them—one filled with happiness and love.

For there was no love at Blackwood Estates, save the love she had for her son, and Caroline had given up hope that Reginald would ever love her. It was not that she had not reached this realization before, but she had taken her vow to remain loyal to her husband seriously even when he did not.

Miss French had remained another evening after the garden incident and then had disappeared for the two days that followed. Now she had returned and was in the company of Reginald once again.

"You are restricted to the sitting room and the gardens," Reginald had informed her. "And your bedroom, of course. Miss French and I have…business to conduct and do not wish to be disturbed." He put his arm around the woman's waist and pulled her close to him, making her giggle.

Any sting such actions would have brought on before no longer did so now. Caroline no longer cared enough to feel jealousy over the women with whom her husband shared his bed. No, even the fact that he flaunted the women in front of her no longer bothered her. He had begun to include Oliver in those flauntings, and that only fueled her anger.

A blind fool could have seen that what Reginald exposed to his son would only twist the boy's mind. That had been the deciding factor to make her escape. If Oliver was forced to grow up under these teachings, she feared that one day he would become as sinister as his father, and she would not allow that to happen.

"Mother," Oliver said, "do you like it?"

Caroline blinked to clear away the cobwebs from her mind. She had come outside to sit on a bench in order to get some air and remove any opportunity for Miss French to wander into the sitting room with one pretense or another. Caroline recognized the woman's propensity to brew up trouble, and trouble was one thing of which Caroline did not need. She now had her plans on which to focus, and any distraction would be detrimental to those plans. She turned to the boy before her, a stem of lilacs in his hand and an expectant look on his face.

"Oh, Oliver, they are beautiful! Are they for me?"

"Yes," the boy replied. "My mother deserves all the best flowers in the world." He thrust the stem toward her, and her heart warmed.

She put the flowers to her nose and breathed deeply. "Oh, they are quite lovely," she said. "What a nice thing to do for me."

The boy gave her a proud grin. "I like to do nice things for you." Then he glanced around, lowered his voice, and cupped his hand beside his mouth. "Father wants me to be nice to Miss French, but I don't like her much. I think she's mean."

"How so?"

"She calls me a nuisance. Why doesn't Father tell her off as he does you?"

It was difficult to maintain her smile, for her heart was caught in her throat. She could never tell the boy, at least not at such a young age, that his father was not a good person.

It would not be until he was much older, and by then he more than likely would see that for himself. Now, he wished to ease the boy's worry.

"Your Father cares." The words attempted to choke her as she said them, but she pressed forward. "He has just been busy as of late."

She feared that Oliver would reject her excuse, but to her delight, the boy nodded.

Oliver turned and smiled, and Caroline followed his gaze to see what had brought on such a reaction.

Philip stood clipping a hedge not far from where she sat. The man had been kind to her that day the previous week, but he had not overstepped his bounds in any way since. He had a gift for gardening, and he completed his work admirably. She was glad he kept his distance; she liked the man—he had been kind to her—and she did not want to see him lose his position if the duke found them speaking to one another when he was in one of his moods.

"I like him," Oliver stated. "He is always nice to me. Can he be my father instead of Father?"

"Oliver Hayward!" Caroline gasped. "Do not say such things ever again. You have a father."

The boy lowered his head. "I'm sorry."

She ruffled his hair and smiled. "Run along and play. Dinner will be soon."

The boy nodded and then turned and walked over to Philip. The two talked, and then Philip patted Oliver on his back.

He will make a good father one day, she thought. Letting out a sigh, she wished that one day she could find a worthy husband. A man who made those around him feel welcome with just his smile—that is, what she could see of his face. She imagined it was a handsome face, although she had yet to see it outright, and she wondered why he allowed his hair to nearly conceal it.

Rising from the bench, she walked over to the gardener as he turned his attention to a large oak tree.

As she approached, Philip stopped and bowed. "Your Grace."

"Did I not request you call me Caroline?" she asked. "At least in private?"

"You did," he replied with a nod. "May I do something for you?"

"You may. I wish to see your face, for it is always concealed behind your hair."

He laughed. "I do not wish to argue with you, but may I ask why?"

"You may ask, but I do not have to reply. Regardless you must do as I say anyway." She tried to hide her mirth but failed miserably.

It was quiet for a moment, and she wondered if he was going to defy her. This, of course, only increased her curiosity. Was he hiding something behind his hair? She had not seen any sign of deformity, nor had any of the servants gossiped about it—not in her presence, that is.

Finally, he brought his hand up and pulled back the dark hair. Her breath caught in her throat, for he had to be one of the most handsome men she had ever seen. He had a defined jawline, a slightly upturned nose, and eyes the color of a stormy sky, and she felt a strange heat in the pit of her stomach she had never felt before.

"Thank you, Mr. Butler."

He gave her an amused smile and allowed his hair to fall back over his face, which she found disappointing. Not only was he handsome, but he also had a kindness about him, and for a moment, she considered telling him of her plans to escape. Perhaps she could even enlist his aid. Not as a love interest, of course, but as someone to help look after her and Oliver.

The notion was foolish. She did not know him. Furthermore, she was a married woman, at least she was in writing. Even having thoughts of spending intimate time with another man without the express consent of her husband would be wrong in the eyes of the law, and her own. She was not a trollop like Miss French, willing to give herself to any man who offered himself to her.

She laughed to herself. What a silly woman she was. The man had not even offered her a cup of tea let alone himself! Yet, he had offered her water…

"Of course, Your Grace," Philip said. "That is why the branches grow so strong. The art of pruning is a tedious, but necessary, task."

Caroline scrunched her brow, wondering what the man meant, but then a voice behind her gave her understanding.

"Do not bore the help with your silly questions," the duke snapped. Then a fit of coughing doubled him over for several moments, a sick, rattling sound. When it subsided, he cleared his throat and added, "Come, dinner will be served soon, and I do not wish to wait." He spoke as if breathing had become difficult, and Caroline felt a pang of concern rush through her. How strange that she should be worried for his health after all he had done. Yet, she was not an uncaring person; even those who did not deserve her concern received it.

She made no comment. "Come. It is time for dinner," she called out to Oliver, who was throwing blades of grass in the air and watching them float to the ground.

"Yes, Mother," the boy replied and came running up to her. He placed his hand in hers as they followed Reginald into the house.

Caroline felt relief wash over her. If the duke had caught her in simple conversation with Philip, his anger would have been great. The kind gardener had saved her once again. And somehow, she found his protection of her endearing, even if the idea of them becoming friends was out of the question.

***

The cough with which the duke suffered continued through that night. Each day after, the hacking increased until the man had to be confined to his bed. He had spoken no words in the past two days, for it only brought on another bout of coughing that took his breath away.

Caroline waited on a chair outside his room while the doctor performed his examination. She wrung her hands as she awaited his findings, unsure if she should be worried or delighted with the fact the man was ill.

No, that was wrong. She was not the type of woman to revel in the sufferings of others, even one such as her husband.

The door opened and Caroline stood.

"Your Grace," the doctor said, his hands clutching his medical bag in front of him, "I'm afraid the prognosis is bleak."

Caroline tilted her head. "Please, tell me plainly."

The man sighed, and for the first time she noticed his reddened eyes and heavy lids. The poor man had been called from his bed in the middle of the night to help with a difficult birth and had only returned home when he was called to Blackwood Estates.

"I am afraid his condition has only worsened. I do not believe he will survive the week. If he is lucky, he will make it two, but certainly no longer. I'm sorry."

Caroline allowed the words to ring in her mind. Although she had every reason to hate her husband, she still felt pity for the man. Even with her recent planning, she did not want to see him suffer, at least not in a physical manner.

"Thank you, Doctor," she said. "I hope you do not think me rude, but if you would see yourself out, I will go to my husband."

He gave her a kind smile. "Of course. And I am sorry to bring you such grave news. If there is anything I can do, please do not hesitate to send for me. I have done all I can to make him as comfortable as possible. If you will excuse me."

"Yes. And thank you again."

He gave her a bow and walked away.

Caroline steeled herself and entered her husband's room. The duke lay in the bed, his face pale and his breathing shallow.

As she neared the bed, a light tap on the door had her turn. Miss French entered without invitation—a symbol of her time at Blackwood Estates—and she carried a large carpet bag, which she had to carry with both hands. She had come with nothing as far as Caroline knew, but the bag appeared quite heavy upon her leaving.

"I have come to say goodbye to Reginald," she said with a sneer.

Caroline narrowed her eyes at the woman. "How dare you…"

"I have every right," Miss French said. "You will have him all to yourself when he dies, so at least allow me to say goodbye."

What Caroline wished was to throw the woman out of the house. If the woman was leaving anyway, what harm could it do?

"Very well, you have two minutes and then you must leave."

Miss French pursed her lips but said nothing as she pushed past Caroline and made her way to the bed. Caroline could not stand to watch, so she walked over to the window, her hands balled into fists at her side.

What was wrong with her? How could she allow this woman to bully her? Yet, she still said nothing.

Exactly two minutes later, Miss French stood, and Caroline followed her into the hallway.

"So, I see you have gotten your greedy hands on the gifts my husband bought for you." Her eyes moved down to the jewels clutched in the woman's hand, much like a desperate thief ready to make her escape.

Miss French responded with a derisive sniff. "I have. I loved him and he loved me." The woman curled her lip. "But what do you care? You care only for yourself."

Caroline understood the game the woman played. "You know your way to the door; see to it that you never enter it again."

With a shake to her head, Miss French turned and headed down the hallway, her slippered steps hushed by the carpeted stairs as she made her way down them. The slamming of the front door was the only indication that the woman had left.

With a sigh, Caroline returned to the bedroom. The frail figure of the duke in his bed was highlighted by the main candles that lit his room. He never liked the darkness, had always insisted on having as many lights lit as he could whenever nighttime came. It was daytime now, the sky covered in dark clouds, though the room was nowhere near dark. Perhaps it was his fear of that eternal darkness that awaited him that had him asking for candles to be lit.

Moving to the wash basin, Caroline rinsed the cloth and returned to the bed. Her husband had fallen back into a fitful sleep and had no reaction to the cold compress she placed on his forehead. The man deserved no mercy nor her care, but enough suffering had been endured in this house and she would allow no more.

As she sat beside him, she wondered at how this man could be so angry with her. His first wife had died young, leaving him with no children, and she suspected that it was because of his loss that he acted as he did. Replacing a love was perhaps too much of a task, something the duke may not have realized until he had married Caroline.

Glancing down, she saw movement. He opened his hand, the first time he had made any physical movement in two days outside of his fits of coughing. She reached down and clasped his hand as his breathing came in short gasps.

"Might you finally find the peace you need," she whispered.

The duke gave her hand a weak squeeze, inhaled, and then his chest stopped moving, never to move again.

Chapter Five

The month after the passing of Reginald Hayward, Duke of Browning, left Caroline with a free spirit, a feeling she had not experienced for many years. Free to say what she pleased. Free to spend as much time with her son as she wished. Free to be herself. She should have been plagued by guilt for allowing such emotions to exist in a time of mourning, but somehow she could not allow herself to worry about it.

She did put on a face of mourning—for the sake of Oliver. The boy had grieved, of course. What child would not grieve for the passing of his father? His spry spirit returned a week later, his cheerful smile and laugh brighter and happier than Caroline had ever seen them.

Now, as the Dowager Duchess of Browning, Caroline found herself in control of a vast empire, through the inheritance of her son, of course. At eight years of age, he would be unable to fulfill those duties. Granted, she had no idea how she would go about preparing Oliver for his eventual responsibilities, but she would do what she could to see him ready and able to assume the title of duke.

"Poor Reginald," Neil lamented beside the fireplace, a glass of brandy in his hand, "I shall miss my brother." He lifted his glass as if to toast the ghost of the former duke and downed it in one go. Then he walked over to the liquor cart and poured himself another, not once asking Caroline if she would like anything other than the tea she had sent for when the man arrived.

Oh, how the man was vile! She wished she could simply throw him out of the house, but the man was her brother-in-law and he had just lost his brother. Who was she to eject a man who was in mourning?

Neil turned to Caroline with that concerned look on his face that seemed so disconcerting to her. "I do feel sorry for Oliver. The poor boy must be beside himself with grief."

"Yes, he does miss his father." It was not a lie; the man had been his father, and although Reginald had never mistreated Oliver personally, the boy had witnessed too often the mistreatment he poured on Caroline.

Lord Hayward sat across from Caroline. The room was opulent, but it was much more garish than Caroline would have liked with its gold velvet chairs and dark wooden tables. It had maintained a manly presence, unlike other sitting rooms which were more feminine in nature. How was a woman to enjoy such a room? Unfortunately, it had not been updated in many years, and most of the décor and furnishings were more than a hundred years old, and if previous dukes had the countenance of Reginald, it was no wonder the women had no say in how the room was decorated.

"Well, I am glad that it is you who will help Oliver grow to the man he must be. He will need extra help in order to take over where his father left off. It is a comfort to know that his inheritance is in good hands." Then he quickly added, "And his future, of course."

This was the second call the man had made on her this week, most of the time lamenting on the loss of his brother. In most cases, this would have been natural, expected;, yet with this man she could not be so certain. What were his intentions? Not once had he placed a compliment on Caroline before—outside of commenting on her beauty or some other forwardness—and if he came to see Reginald, she might as well have been away for all he cared. One thing was certain, his current speech made her uncomfortable.

Neil rose once again. He made a move to return to the liquor cart but turned instead, looking down on her with watery eyes. "Title, wealth, and beauty," he said as he placed his glass back on the table. "You certainly have it all."

She remained silent, wishing the man to say his piece and leave.

He walked around the sofa where she sat to stand behind her. When he placed an arm on her shoulder, she kept herself from shivering with disgust.

"You have no husband and no experience with business," he said, his voice now with an oily tinge to it, like a slippery eel sliding through ocean depths. "How will you ever handle it all?"

"I will learn," Caroline said as she rose from the sofa with the pretense of poking at the low fire.

Moving did not keep him at bay, for when she turned, he stood behind her, close enough to smell the brandy on his breath. He took her hand in hers and said, "Marry me. Allow me to counsel Oliver and secure his future, as well as yours. He will be the next Duke of Browning…nay, he already is. And it is a title that needs a strong, guiding hand."

He took a step closer and wrapped his arms around her waist. Panic welled up inside her, and she tried to move back, but he was too strong. He pulled her to him, pressing his body against hers. "Allow me to take care of you." His voice had an alarming huskiness to it that made her tremble in fear.

The meal Caroline had consumed at midday threatened to discharge itself from her stomach. The man was vile, yes, but the alarm that erupted inside went beyond this man. In her mind's eyes, images of Reginald and his harsh treatment of her flew before her. She had to get away!

Yet, sensibility somehow pressed through. This was not Reginald. This man held no power over her, not like that which her husband had used to beat her down. And as the fear began to dissipate, anger took its place. She wanted nothing more than to slap this man across the face, to show him how his disregard for her, for who she was, made her feel. She tried to push him away, but he only pulled her in tighter.

"You know we would be good together," he whispered. "Marry me, Caroline. I have always wanted you; you should know that." His lips came dangerously close to hers, and she could feel his hot breath on her face.

"Your Grace?" a voice said from the doorway, "I apologize for interrupting, but I was told you needed to see me?"

Neil released Caroline so quickly that she had to catch herself on the arm of the sofa to keep herself from landing on her backside. She looked over, grateful to see Philip, the gardener, standing at the door, his hat in his hands in front of him.

"You fool!" Neil shouted. "Can you not see that Her Grace is engaged in a conversation?" Then he grimaced at the man. "No, of course you cannot, for that wild hair of yours blocks your vision. Go! Leave us at once. Her Grace will be available to speak with you at a later time."

Caroline stepped forward. "He will remain," she said, the fear she had now replaced by a wave of red-hot anger, "and you will leave." How dare this man order her servants as if they were his own? More importantly, how could he even dare to try to kiss her? She would take no more abuse from any man, regardless of who they were!

"You dare throw me out of my brother's home?" Neil said, sputtering with anger. "I am blood! You cannot do this!"

Caroline smiled, her eyes meeting his without a drop of her previous fear. "This home may have belonged to your brother, but it is not yours," she said, surprised at the authority in her voice. "Nor will it ever be. Do not return, or I will have you removed bodily and the story spread about the *ton* that you laid a hand on the widow of your brother."

The man faltered for a moment, his cheeks red with anger. "You will regret this," he said, spittle spraying from his lips. "Fool," he mumbled as he stormed past the gardener, who stood with his head bowed and his hair still covering his face, and out the sitting room door.

When the front door slammed, Philip looked up. "He is gone. Are you safe…Caroline?"

She took a moment to steady herself, for the room had begun to spin precariously around her. The interaction had upset her more than she thought. Taking a deep breath, she replied, "Yes, I believe so." She studied the man who had helped her on more than one occasion. She had not called for him, and yet he had arrived at the exact moment she needed him.

He did not raise his head, and she somehow found herself wanting to push back the curtain of hair that obscured his handsome features.

"How is it you know when I am in danger? It is as if you can sense me."

He smiled down at her through his hair. "Luck," he replied. "Or stupidity. I have not quite decided."

She could not stop herself from laughing. "I promise you that you are not stupid," she said. "For that, I am glad." It was difficult to pull her eyes away from his, but she did so and moved to the seating area. "Please, come share a drink with me. The tea will be cold by now, but you are welcome to a glass of spirits. I have brandy."

"I should not…"

"Oh, come now," she said. "Can I not offer a drink to the man who has saved me not once but thrice?"

He was hesitant, but then he nodded. She poured him a measure of brandy and handed him the glass.

"Thank you," he said in a low voice.

Caroline walked over and sat on the sofa, offering him the place beside her. Rather than accepting that spot, he took a seat in the chair Neil had vacated. Well, if that was what he preferred, she would not argue with the man.

"Neil sought my hand in marriage," she said with a laugh. "Can you believe such a thing?"

"I can," he replied without hesitation—and without mirth.

"You can?" she asked in shock.

"Yes. It will not only be him, but other men will soon be looking to win your heart. Your title and wealth will call to the vultures. He is not the last, for many more will come."

"That title and wealth does not belong to me," she said with a laugh.

He gave her a half-smile. "No, it is that of your son. And how long will it be before he is old enough to take on the responsibilities of that title?" He did not wait for her to reply. "Many years. Therefore, men will come in droves to weasel their way into your life, even if they are only able to enjoy the benefits of your son's money for a relatively short time."

"Oh, so what you are saying, then, is that men only seek my attention because I now have wealth?"

His cheeks reddened. "Well, no, for you are a beautiful woman; that alone would cause a man to seek your favor." He cleared his throat and looked back down, his hair once again returning to cover his face. "I am sorry. I have spoken out of turn."

Caroline took a drink of the brandy she had poured for herself hoping to ease the sudden flushed feeling that had come over her. She hoped she was not falling ill. Yet, she had been under a lot of stress as of late. Yes, that would explain the strange warmness she was feeling.

"No, Philip, you have not spoken out of turn," she replied. "I find myself now in control of things about which I know nothing, and then the brother of my husband comes with his brazen ideas to win me over. With me in my mourning period and the need to learn the ways of business before someone decides to take advantage of my lack of knowledge, I admit that I am more than a bit overwhelmed."

"Your husband had no bookkeeper? No one who took care of his finances?"

Caroline shook her head. "No. He once told me that he did not trust anyone with his books. He said that if he did not take care of them himself, anyone could cheat him out of every farthing and he would not know the difference." She sighed. "Should I hire a tutor in such matters? Or would it be better if I simply handed it all over to an accountant or some other person who deals in such matters?"

"I do not believe I am the one to advise you in such matters," he said in a low voice. "I am merely a simple gardener, and there are those who are far better suited."

Caroline sighed. "This might be true, and yet I trust no one here, save Quinton. And you." She gave him a beseeching look. "It was you who risked everything to give me water when you were told explicitly not to do so, and I have not forgotten that kind gesture. So, now I must ask you again, what shall I do?"

Philip seemed to study the brandy, which he had yet to drink. It took him several moments before he spoke, and Caroline worried he would not respond at all.

"If you would allow me to look at your ledgers, I can advise you."

Caroline's eyes widened. This was not what she had expected. What she had expected was that he would suggest a bookkeeper or other person practiced in that area. Had he not just said he was only a simple gardener? Yet what other choice did she have?

She walked over to a small desk in the corner and retrieved a stack of papers. "The solicitors gave me this," she said as she handed them to Philip. "The ledgers on the shelf contain more information."

Philip set his glass on a side table and came to stand beside her. It was strange, but his nearness made her knees weak. Or was it that midday meal again? She once again felt a burning feeling throughout her body, but she knew it was not a fever. Strange.

"May I look over the papers?" he asked.

She looked down and realized that she still held what she had been given by the solicitors. With a nod of her head, she handed him the information and then hurried back over to the seating area. Pouring herself a cup of tea, she drank the entire glass to quench her parched throat. As she had suspected, it was cold.

Philip moved his hair back over an ear and studied the paperwork, his lips moving slightly as he read in a most endearing manner. How handsome he looked standing there by the desk, as if he belonged there.

Caroline was unsure as to what she should do while she waited. Oliver was busy with his studies, and she thought it best to remain here watching over Philip. It would never do to leave the gardener alone in the sitting room, would it? It had nothing to do with her wanting to watch him. At least that is what she told herself as she took a drink of the brandy she had not even noticed that she had picked up off the table.

***

Caroline had not considered herself one for enjoying the drinking of spirits, but she found herself enjoying it as she watched Philip. He had finally sat in the chair in front of the desk after pulling first one ledger and then another from the shelf and reading through them as if reading a book. The way he studied the pages as he turned them was somehow…alluring.

She giggled as she looked down at her glass, the third thus far, much to her surprise. It was time to stop, for she would make a fool of herself as well as embarrass the poor man.

"The books have been well-kept," he said finally. "All his affairs seem to be in order. You have properties in town as well as in London and Bath. Most of the fortune was made in those properties; although it seems that shipping has been the main focus as of late."

She had known about the properties in town, as well as London. "Bath? I did not realize he had property in Bath." She rose and stood to gaze down at the page full of numbers, none of it making sense to her.

Philip nodded. "It appears he has property with several cottages on a large plot of land there. The tenants all pay their rents on time, and it brings in a nice sum."

"Please, go on."

"Well, with the income from the real estate alone, you and Oliver will never have to worry about anything. As I said, there are the rents in Bath, but most of the properties in London are storefronts, which bring in an even larger sum of money." He closed the ledger in front of him. "You have enough money coming in to not only maintain this home, but it will also afford to buy any luxury you desire. Taking into account the money and his business ventures in shipping, Oliver's grandchildren should never want for anything. If it is managed properly, of course."

Caroline let out a relieved sigh and placed her hand on Philip's arm, surprised at the muscles beneath the sleeves of his shirt. He gave a slight tremor, as if her touch pained him, and she withdrew her hand. What had she been thinking, putting her hands on the man?

"You have explained what I could not understand," she said. Then a new thought came to her. "How is it that you speak so eloquently and are so educated?"

"For a gardener, you mean?"

Her cheeks burned. "Yes," she whispered, embarrassed that she would have been so rude.

He chuckled, seeming to not be offended by her words. "Like you, I was fortunate enough to have things taught to me."

She could not help but be curious about his past. That would come later, if at all. He was her gardener, after all, not a man she should be asking intimate questions about his life. "Do you suggest I find someone to manage the estate for me?"

He leaned back in the chair and pulled his hair back over his ear once again, silent for a moment. Then he said, "There are those in town who are of good repute. There is the Baxter family. My advice would be to allow Marcus Baxter to manage your holdings. Not that I believe you could not do it yourself if given proper instruction; however, for their cost versus the time it would allow you to spend time with your son and attend to your duties as the Dowager Duchess, it would be a wise decision."

Caroline smiled. "You save me from thirst, protect me from those who seek to use me for their own gain, and guide me in business. I have promised to repay you three times, and yet you still ask for nothing in return?"

He rose from the chair, their bodies less than a hands-width apart. As he looked down on her, she thought her knees would buckle beneath her.

"I do not seek any payment," he said quietly. "I only ask that you allow me to remain here working on your grounds. I need nothing more."

Caroline stared up at him, and that feeling of freedom returned. She was now free to make her own decisions. She knew nothing of the world, yet this man did. He was kind and generous with his knowledge, and although she could not explain the reason, behind those soft, blue eyes she could see he would never hurt or use her in any way.

"I cannot have you as my gardener anymore," she whispered. "I need you as my protector. Someone who can escort me into town, to keep me safe from men who seek my hand only as a means to reach my son's wealth. And to advise me when I need strength. Will you do this for me?"

He rubbed his chin and seemed to consider her offer. "There are those who would be far more suitable for such a position," he said finally. "It would be wise to choose someone other than your gardener."

She smiled as she returned her hand to his arm. This time the trembling was not there. "It is because of that advice that I want you," she said. She knew her cheeks had to be bright red, for her face was aflame. "Will you accept?"

He was silent for a moment before replying, and she found herself holding her breath. Was she doing the right thing in asking a man of his standing to advise her? What did a gardener know, truly, of running an estate the size of Blackwood Estates? Deep in her heart, she knew he was the right man.

"I accept," he finally whispered, and Caroline reveled in his words, knowing she had, indeed, made the right decision.

Chapter Six

Life was strange, or so thought Philip as he walked along the garden path. He had risen two hours earlier, and although he was no longer the gardener for the estate, he could not stop himself from being out among the flowers and trees that had become his life for so long. How strange that he had come to find employment here at Blackwood Estates with thoughts of completing a single task.

Yet, that plan was jeopardized when he accepted the request Caroline had made the night before. It was not that he did not wish to come to the woman's aid, for she clearly needed guidance, but he was not the man to help her, as he had mentioned to her before.

He sighed. In all honesty, it was more than that; it was because he had grown especially fond of the woman. Unsure when it had happened, for he had not recognized it for what it was until it was much too late, he tried to suppress those old feelings he had long since buried, and he did not have it in him to experience them anytime soon. Not for his sake, but for hers.

To fall in love again would be more than a bit inconvenient, and he did not wish to give Caroline the wrong impression. She had no love for her husband, and he knew she would seek it, even if she could not see it as so.

It was in her eyes, clouded with torment, that she was in need of a healing touch. How he wished to be the one to ease that pain, to remove her hurts and in the process removing his own.

He possessed an agony so great, a loss so deep, that it was not a journey he wished to take again. For at the end of his current journey, only more pain awaited him. And if he grew close to her, she would learn of what he had done, would learn about his past, and he could not allow that life to touch her.

Timid footsteps approached from behind, and he smiled. "Your steps are loud," he said without turning. Caroline laughed, and he cursed himself inwardly for enjoying it.

"How is it you have the hearing of a fox?" she asked. "Tell me, were you raised in the forest?" She came to stand beside him.

He looked over and soaked in her beauty. The yellow dress set off her blond tresses, and the tiny brown flowers matched her eyes. He could look at her for hours if he was given the chance to do so.

"The secret is out, then," he said, keeping a serious expression on his face. "I was raised in a forest by a band of hermits led by a fox."

The tinkling laugh almost made him break into a smile. "Oh, Philip, you are so silly."

He glanced at her, maintaining the solemn appearance, and she took a step back.

"Were you really raised by them?" she asked in shock.

"Indeed. For years, I was forced to hunt wild game at night with my bare hands." He raised his hands toward her as if they were claws. "During the day, I read books."

Her eyes widened, and he had to fight back another laugh.

"Then, when women such as yourself came along in the woods…"

"Yes?" she whispered, her expectation clear.

"I would bark like a dog at them."

This made them both laugh, and she playfully slapped at his arm again. "You almost had me convinced; although, I do not see you as that wild man you tried to portray. No, you are far better than that, far more domesticated."

He gave her a smile. To know that such a creature as the one who stood before him thought of him as something better than he appeared was a great compliment.

"I know very little about you," she continued. "You are a man of few words, and I cannot have you guarding me without knowing something about you."

Worry washed over him, for he had no desire to speak of his past, and the thought of lying to this woman made him uncomfortable.

She did not seem to notice his discomfort. "Therefore, you will accompany me into town today. While I am speaking to Mr. Baxter about business, I would like you to see to having new clothes ordered."

"Caroline," he said, raising his hand. "You are kind, but I cannot accept such a gift."

"You would defy your duchess?" she demanded in a haughty tone.

He chuckled. "You know I would not do such a thing."

"Good. You will purchase one set of ready-made clothing so you can dine with Oliver and me as our honored guest this evening. I would also like you to see the tailor and have at least three suits made. It would not do to have you wearing the same clothing you wore as a gardener now that you have been promoted to a new position."

Nothing could have stopped the smile that spread across his face, yet it was not for receiving new clothing.

"And at what do you smile?" she asked.

"You," came his reply. "It is nice to see you smile again. I feared it would be something I would never see."

She sighed. "I must admit, I feared very much the same for a very long time."

***

Oliver had remained at home to complete his lessons for the day as Philip and Caroline rode into town an hour earlier. Philip had already purchased clothing for dinner as Caroline had requested, and an order had been taken by the tailor after one of the man's helpers gathered Philip's measurements. It was strange to have such attention paid to him, and he was glad to now be on his way to meet Caroline outside of Baxter and Sons.

As he neared the offices, he smiled when the Dowager Duchess exited the building, the sun catching the highlights in the wisps of hair that peeked out from her bonnet. He could not believe what a beautiful creature she was—and how fortunate he was to be in her company. Granted, it was as her employee, but that was enough for him.

"How did it go?" he asked when he came to stand beside her.

She smiled. "Extremely well. I have hired the company to attend to all of the business matters. Mr. Baxter, the father that is, was such a kind man." She tilted her head at him. "But when I spoke of you, he did not seem to recognize your name."

Philip laughed. "Are you surprised he did not know the name of your gardener?" he asked with amusement. "The fact of the matter is, previous employers have spoken of him; that is how I knew to come to him."

"I see," Caroline said with a nod. Then she sighed heavily. "Oh, bother. These two women coming toward us are nothing but a couple of gossips. I do not wish to speak to them."

Philip grinned as he watched the women approach. Blond curls lined both of their youthful faces, and Philip could just make out one set of blue eyes and one set of brown beneath the shade of the hats they wore.

The two women stopped in front of Caroline, and the first, whose blue dress matched her eyes perfectly, said, "Oh, Your Grace, we were so sorry to hear of the death of your husband." She spoke with exaggerated concern and brought her hand to her breast dramatically.

Philip could see that what Caroline had said was true; the moment these women left her presence, anything she said would be spread far and wide.

"Such pain you must be suffering," the second said with much solicitude as she spoke over her friend, her green dress dotted with tiny white daisies swishing around her feet. "Surely you will be wanting to host a party to express your heartbreak."

Caroline replied with a small nod.

Philip cleared his throat, and both women gave an intake of breath as they turned to look at him. "Ladies," he said with a small bow, "my name is Philip Butler, and I am Her Grace's protector."

The woman in the blue dress leaned in toward her companion and whispered, "I did not know she had a protector," she said, as if she did not realize he could hear what she was saying. Then to Philip she said, "I am Miss Barnsworthy. This is my friend, Miss Cuplin, and we have been acquainted with the Duchess for some years now."

Philip stifled a chuckle. "Be that as it may, Her Grace has been distraught, and rightly so."

Both women nodded. "But of course she would be," Miss Cuplin replied. "She has lost her husband. Any woman would be distraught if she were in her position."

"I am glad you understand," Philip replied. "In her current state, she would like me to pass on something to those such as yourselves."

"Of course," Miss Barnsworthy said. "Anything that can help ease her pain."

Philip gave them a smile. "To quote her exact words: 'Due to the untimely death of His Grace, the Duke of Browning, and my husband, I have decided to take on a vow of silence for the next few months. Please do not count my lack of words or rejections of any events as rude but rather as a time for me to attempt to heal the wounds in my heart as well as in that of our son, Oliver.'" He bowed deeper when he finished.

Miss Cuplin pulled a kerchief from a cuff and dabbed at her eye. "That is the most beautiful gesture," she said. "May we pass on this knowledge to others?"

"That would please Her Grace and, of course, find you in her favor."

Both women grinned like schoolgirls who had received top marks.

"Now, if you will excuse us, we must be on our way." He gave the women one more bow before offering Caroline his arm. She placed her hand on it and the two walked away, the admiration of the women clear in the reflection of a nearby window.

"I believe six months is an adequate amount of time to keep you free from the prying interests of women and the hands of men who seek yours only for their gain." He said. "I hope you do not mind."

"Philip Butler," she said with a wide grin, "of course, I do not mind!" They approached the waiting carriage, and Philip opened the door. Before stepping up, Caroline shared another of her wonderful smiles with him. "You amaze me every day. I consider myself lucky to have a friend such as yourself."

Although he wished to tell her the same, he knew he could not. "I am glad to be of service," he said instead and then helped her into the carriage.

Perhaps one day he would be able to share with her what was on his heart, but for now, it was enough to simply be in her presence.

***

The smell of roast lamb in wine sauce made Philip's stomach grumble. He would have found it less embarrassing if Oliver had not giggled at him, clearly having heard it and finding it amusing as oftentimes young boys did. Caroline did not seem to notice, much to Philip's relief. The candles lit her face, and she smiled widely as she lifted her wine glass to him.

"Thank you for joining us this evening," she said.

"And I thank you for the invitation," Philip replied, also lifting his glass to her.

"Mr. Butler," Oliver said as he sat across from Philip on Caroline's right hand, "have you ever gone fishing before?"

"Yes, I have, young master," Philip replied. "Do you enjoy it?"

The boy shrugged. "I don't know. I want to go, but I'm not sure how to go about it. Could you teach me?"

His innocent brown eyes, looking very much like his mother's, made it difficult for Philip to deny the boy his request.

Yet, he should, for he feared a growing attachment to the boy. To find himself separated from both the boy and his mother would be unbearable.

Caroline was appalled. "Oliver, you should not be asking such things of Mr. Butler. He has other tasks with which to concern himself. He does not need to be traipsing after a young boy who is not in his care."

Oliver lowered his head. "I'm sorry."

Philip set his fork on his plate and looked at Caroline through his hair. He still could not get himself to look at her directly. "I will honor any request you make of me," he said meaningfully.

"Very well," she replied after a moment of thought. "Tomorrow, after your studies, of course, you may go fishing, and Mr. Butler will accompany you. But you must give Miss Lindston your gravest attention."

The boy nodded emphatically. "I will, Mother. I promise!" He returned to his dinner with fervor, clearly excited for the following day's activities.

When everyone appeared to have eaten as much as they could, Caroline turned to Oliver and said, "Miss Lindston will see you to bed. I will be up shortly to read you a story."

Oliver pushed his chair back. "Yes, Mother," he said and then went to allow his mother to place a kiss on his cheek. Then he turned to Philip. "Thank you for taking me fishing tomorrow, Mr. Butler."

"I am honored," Philip replied, and the boy bounded out of the room and up the stairs, the voice of the governess following after him that he should walk and not run.

"He is a fine young man," Philip said as he went to pull the chair out for Caroline.

When she turned to look at him, their eyes met for a moment, and he turned away, using the need to push his chair back under the table as an excuse.

"I do not understand why you hide behind this hair," she whispered as she pushed his hair away from his face. "It is much too handsome a face to be kept hidden. Why not bind it with a ribbon at the nape of your neck; it is what most men do these days.

Then everyone will be able to see your face and you could maintain the length."

Her nearness made breathing difficult, and he had to force air from his lungs to produce words to speak. "There is nothing I will not do for you," he said. "Save one." He pushed his long hair back over his shoulder. "Allow me to wear it like this, for it gives me comfort."

She pulled back, hurt in her eyes. He had not meant to upset her, but somehow his request had done so.

"Might I ask why?" she said. Then she waved a hand in the air. "No, it is not for me to force you to explain. I do not wish to interfere." She went to turn, but he reached and caught her arm.

"Like you," he explained, "I carry much pain. Unlike your pain, mine is of my own doing."

She turned back to face him. "I understand," she said in a soft voice filled with kindness. "I did not mean to pry. But thank you for sharing at least that small piece with me." She raised herself onto her toes and kissed his cheek. "Thank you, Philip. Sleep well."

And with that, she turned and walked away.

When she was gone, Philip released a frustrated sigh and walked over to the window that overlooked the garden. How he wanted to chase after her and assure himself she had not been hurt by his stubbornness. To hold her and perhaps even kiss her. He was not deserving of such attention; she deserved so much better.

For the last time he had loved a woman, she had died, and her blood had stained his hands. It was for the guilt of that moment that he kept his face covered. Yet, how did one explain such horrors to a woman such as Caroline Hayward?

Chapter Seven

As it so happened, Philip and Oliver convinced Caroline to join them on their fishing expedition, Oliver on the verge of begging and Philip…well, he simply asked. Caroline could not have declined if she had tried in either case.

"Here, allow me to help," Philip said, offering his hand as her foot slipped on the wet grass.

Caroline stared at the hand for several moments, unsure whether taking his hand would be appropriate or not. What would have been worse, someone seeing the man aid her in climbing a steep hill or her falling flat on her backside? Therefore, she grabbed his hand, and he pulled her up to the top of the grassy hill.

They had decided to walk the short distance to a small dock that Reginald had built on the river that ran through the property. There, the water pooled, and according to Philip, they would have many fish from which to choose.

Oliver had been amazed at this. "Is that where they live, then?" he had asked, his eyes wide with innocence.

"Indeed," Philip replied. "We should have great success in our hunt."

"Hunt?" Oliver said with a boisterous laugh. "We are not hunting! We are fishing! And won't we be leaving the fish in the river rather than eating them?"

Philip raised his eyebrows. "Is that not why we go fishing?"

Oliver shook his head as if Philip was the one who did not know things. "Of course not. We're there to catch them, but we can't take them away from their families. They'd be sad. And wouldn't you be sad if you were playing along in the water and something caught you and ate you?"

Philip laughed. "I suppose I would at that." Then he ruffled the boy's hair.

Caroline had watched this interaction from behind them and had been mystified—and perhaps even a bit pleased—at how compatible the two were.

"There it is!" Oliver shouted. Indeed, the small wooden dock protruded out over the pooled water, a clear expanse that reflected the sky above. "I will go and see if I can find any fish!" Without waiting for a response, the boy was rushing down the hill toward the water.

Caroline went to shout at the boy lest he fall, but Philip let out a small chuckle.

"He will be fine," the man said. "You must realize that boys are prone to falling and hurting themselves, but they always continue on despite these mishaps."

She gave a sigh. "You are right, of course," she said. "I worry too much over him these days, for I fear harm will come to him. He is all I have left."

"No harm will come to him," Philip replied.

Not understanding why, she believed what he said. It was as if his words possessed some sort of magical power, a source of enchantment in some way. But that was a ridiculous thought!

"You two go ahead," she said with a sigh. "I will set up here." The cook had prepared a basket as Caroline went in search of a large blanket they could spread upon the grass so they could have a place to eat. She had also added a book to the basket so she would have something to do whilst the men set about with their fishing.

The weather was perfect with just the slightest wisps of clouds in the sky and a warmness to the air. Springtime in Devin had to be the best time of the year as far as Caroline was concerned, for it held promises of days to come.

It was not only the weather that had Caroline smiling. The fact of the matter was that she had never seen Oliver so filled with joy, even before the passing of his father. For the first time in his short life, the boy romped and played like so many other boys his age.

Whether or not it was the case for all boys bound for dukedom to have them kept wrapped in cotton wool, she did not know, but she had seen many a boy from the small village from whence she came gallivanting around in the fields behind the cottage her parents owned. She had forgotten about the happiness of children, or what should have been as such. Until now. And that smile her son wore today could only be attributed to one man. Philip Butler.

Philip was a quiet man, reserved, at least with Caroline. She was able to see snippets of who the man truly was by observing his interactions with Oliver, for he was much more animated, more playful, than he was in her company.

The fact he did not share this inner person with her did not perturb her—everyone was allowed his or her secrets—but somehow, she wished he would show such openness with her. When he shared even the smallest of details with her, the act made her feel special in some way, as if he had given her a gift of some sort.

She flicked out the blanket and set it on the ground beneath a large oak tree where she could be well-shaded and watch Oliver. Once everything was set up just as she wanted, she sat down, spread out her skirts around her, and regarded the two by the pool. Philip was instructing the boy on how to hold his wooden rod, flicking it back and forth and then having Oliver imitate. Philip was patient answering every question Oliver asked without flying into a fury as the boy's father might have done.

Reaching into the basket, she removed a bottle of wine and poured herself a small amount in one of the glasses the cook had included, relishing the moment. Reginald never would have come out with them; he never had time for either them, not to do something as frivolous as picnicking and fishing. He never spoke words of affection to his son, only commands, and here was this man, a gardener by trade, treating Oliver as his own son.

A thought crossed her mind, and she allowed her imagination to take her to a place where Philip was her husband and a father to Oliver. He was handsome, especially so, and his heart was gentle. Yet, she could sense a strong man buried inside, a man who would protect rather than hurt her.

Each day as Oliver finished his studies, Philip would greet him, praise him for his hard work. Together, as a family, they would dine, and after Oliver was sent off to bed, Philip would wrap his arms around her. As he would hold her tightly, he would lean down and press his lips to hers. Any cares she might have, he would ease with his lips and his heart. And for the first time in her life, she would feel the love of a man.

A loud laugh brought her back to the present, and she shook her head to clear it of such ridiculous thoughts. Love was a foreign concept to her, one she would not recognize if it fell into her lap. How, then, would she imagine herself being inflicted with such an ailment?

Therefore, she turned her thoughts to the man himself and she found herself wondering if he had ever been in love before. Was it even appropriate to ask such a question of the man she had asked to be her protector?

"The boy is a fast learner," Philip said as he came to tower over her. "Would you mind if I joined you?"

Caroline laughed. "Of course not," she replied. "Please, have a seat. Would you like a glass of wine?"

He took a moment to answer before nodding. "Yes, that would be nice."

She poured for him and then handed him the glass.

"You seemed lost in thought," he said after thanking her for the wine.

She nodded and worried her lower lip as she watched Oliver standing like a soldier at attention at the edge of the dock. "Only the thoughts of a woman, so you would find it quite silly."

He laughed. "There are women who are foolish, I would agree, though I can promise you that you are not one of them."

Her cheeks burned and she took another sip of her wine to cool herself. "That is kind of you to say," she said when she was able to speak again. "I often think of my marriage to the duke and how it was not for love. To be honest, I wonder what love is like."

He said nothing as he studied his wine, and she realized that she had become much too personal with this man, more than likely causing him embarrassment.

"My apologies. Please realize that I have no friends, no family other than Oliver. Reginald forbade me from seeing anyone outside of the home. In the beginning, some of my old friends came to call, but they rarely returned. The only interaction I have with people besides my servants is when we have a party, and that certainly is no place to be with friends close enough in which to confide."

"Never apologize to me, Caroline," he said quietly, "for you have done no wrong. As to your question, love is something one must experience to understand it."

She nodded as she watched a bird settle onto a branch above them. "That raven is a sign of love. That is what it is."

Philip looked up. "I do not understand. A raven is love? I thought love was restricted to doves."

Caroline laughed. "Not at all. Allow me to explain."

"Please do, for I am confused."

"You see, there is a story I heard once about a man called the Duke of Ravens. Are you familiar with it?"

He shook his head.

"Well, many years ago, when I was but a girl of thirteen, a man's wife and daughter were kidnapped. Sadly, those who took them killed them once they received the ransom. The duke sought after those who took the people he loved and tracked down every single one of them. They say the love he had for his family was so strong, the ravens of the sky followed him overhead throughout the forest, calling down to him as they led him to where the kidnappers hid. With their powers, he was able to avenge their deaths, thus solidifying the love he had for his wife." She let out a sigh and finished the remaining wine in her glass. "Love so strong that even the animals helped him seek his revenge."

"Quite the story," Philip said with a chuckle. "Have you met this man?"

"No. From what I have heard, he returned to his estate and has never left again. To this day, he remains there, heartbroken and alone, with only the ravens to visit him and console him. It is beautiful, do you not believe so?"

Philip handed the glass to her and stood. "It is a lovely tale; although, I must admit it does sound a bit far-fetched. Perhaps it is the meaning of the story that keeps the story alive rather than it being truth, much like tales of fairies and giants." With that, he walked away.

Caroline was unsure what to think of his assessment of a story she held dear to her. Although the man might have been right that it was just a folktale meant to encourage, she still found it beautiful. Furthermore, it gave her hope that such men existed, that not all men were driven by greed or lust but rather by love.

Guilt plagued her for the thoughts of Philip she had experienced, so she poured herself another glass of wine and opened her book to lose herself into a realm of make-believe.

***

"I must say, Your Grace, your gown is beautiful." Margaret, Caroline's lady's maid, was the only thing besides Oliver that Reginald had unwittingly gotten right. If he ever learned how complimentary the woman was, he would have seen her replaced as soon as possible by another less agreeable servant, or so thought Caroline.

"Thank you," Caroline said, giving the woman a smile. "It is one of the new ones I ordered last month."

The woman took a pin and added to her coiffure. "Well, it is very becoming on you, if I may say so."

Caroline blushed. Accepting compliments had never been easy, but after what she had endured the past five years made doing so that much more difficult.

"Will you be having a guest tonight?" Margaret asked. The older woman was keen to nose about in other's business, and Caroline found it endearing. She was not loose of tongue like most women, therefore making speaking with her much easier.

"Philip will be dining with us," she replied. "Oliver has taken a liking to him."

Margaret set another pin. "He's a nice man, and if I were ten years younger, I believe I'd never stop seeking his attentions." Then she gasped. "I'm sorry for speaking that way! I don't know what came over me."

Caroline laughed. "You are fine. He is a handsome man; I have taken notice of that."

"Oh, my, yes. Handsome he is for sure."

"I also find I enjoy his company, but I fear he finds me quite boring."

Margaret clicked her tongue. "Nonsense. I don't believe it. No one would be able to find you boring."

"I have tried to induce conversation with him during the various activities we have done together—not to win his affections, of course."

"Of course," Margaret echoed, although she did not seem convinced.

"I would simply like him to reveal more about himself. He is a quiet man."

"That he is," Margaret agreed. "Some men can't seem to refrain from talking too much and others are brooders. He's somewhere in between, from what I've gathered. He seems to choose his words wisely." She set the last pin and took a step back to assess her handiwork. "There. What do you think?"

Caroline turned this way and that as she checked her reflection in the mirror. "Yes, your work is perfect, as usual." She turned to face her maid. "Margaret, if you were to want to learn more about a man, what would you do to get him to open up more?"

The woman sighed. "I don't rightly know," she said. Then she shrugged. "I suppose loads of drink would loosen a stiff tongue."

Caroline gasped. "I cannot do that!"

"He's your protector, isn't he?"

Caroline nodded.

"Then he has to travel wherever you go, am I right?"

With another nod, Caroline replied, "You are."

"Then I suggest you go on holiday."

"Holiday," Caroline mumbled. "Yes, that is a good idea."

"To be honest, Your Grace, you haven't really left this estate in years. It would do you good to get out to see and experience new things."

Caroline pondered the woman's words. She had estates all over the country, most she had never visited. It was true that she had been cooped up in the house since Reginald's passing, and even before that, she had only been allowed to leave when he escorted her to a party or dinner. Time away would be good for her and Oliver. Plus, it would give her time with Philip, away from prying eyes.

"Thank you, Margaret," she said, placing a hand on the woman's hand. "I will ask him tonight if he will accompany me." She quickly added, "as my protector, of course."

"Of course," Margaret replied, though her smile never faltered.

Chapter Eight

A fortnight later, Caroline found herself sitting on a grassy hill overlooking the ocean, a sight she had never seen before. Above her, the sky was a deep blue, and below her, white crests topped the waves.

She had arrived in Cornwall the day before, tired from the long journey and yet still excited to experience something new. Oliver was napping, Miss Lindston watching over him, and Philip was beside her, watching over Caroline.

"Is there anything in particular that you would like to do while we are here?" he asked. His voice had a formal tone to it, but they had been inside the carriage for so long, she could imagine that he had developed a habit of formality with her.

"The ocean," she said, "This is my first experience with it. Might we go closer?"

"Of course," he replied. He stood and then offered his hand, which she took without hesitation.

She slipped her arm in his, and they made their way down the hill.

"I thought the boy would be too excited to sleep," Philip said.

"As did I. Although, I must admit, I find I am quite tired myself; I am just too stubborn to allow sleep to win." This brought on a shared laughter that made Caroline feel warm inside.

They came to a path that led down to a sandy beach, and Caroline smiled at the other couples, who, like she and Philip, walked together arm in arm.

Yet, she did not feel a sense of satisfaction at the thought. "We are not a couple," she whispered to herself as a reminder of where they stood.

Philip glanced down at her. "Did you say something?"

"No," she said much too quickly. "Well, I mean, yes. I was just reciting a line of poetry." A strange twinge of guilt came to her, yet to tell this man the truth of what she had said could not happen, so she resigned herself to the lie.

The sand beneath her slippered feet crumbled as they continued their trek forward, and they finally came to a stop.

"It is truly magnificent," she said. "In all my life, I never thought I would be blessed enough to see the ocean, and yet, here I am." She closed her eyes and inhaled deeply, enjoying the salty scent in the air and the cool breeze that touched her skin.

"Now that you are here, then, that dream is realized," Philip said.

She opened her eyes and looked up at him. "True, but I still have many more dreams. Will they be fulfilled, as well, my wise friend?"

"I believe they will."

They remained quiet for a short time, and Caroline found that just watching the waves brought about a sense of peace, as did the man beside her. His presence alone made her feel safe, and she was glad he was there with her.

"I told you before that I do not have any friends," she said as she turned her gaze out to the ocean waves once again. "And although you are my protector and I am your employer, I do consider you a friend."

Philip remained quiet, and she worried she had offended him in some way. It was strange, but she found his silence disappointing.

When he did speak, he seemed to choose his words carefully. "Once you are set into your new life, you will have new friends, far better friends than your gardener. I will not be around forever."

His words crushed her heart, and she wondered why she found them so cruel. "So, you plan on leaving me one day?" she asked, attempting to mask the hurt in her voice but knowing she failed.

"It is inevitable." He turned to look down at her once again. "Yet it will not be because it is something I want."

She found his words evasive. "Then why would you leave?

He sighed. "Because life gives us unexpected turns. What we believe will happen tomorrow might not. One day, you will meet a man who will capture your heart. Your attention will turn to him, as it should. When that happens, my presence will no longer be needed, nor will it be appropriate."

Without explanation, anger rose in Caroline. "I will decide what is appropriate," she snapped. "Not my gardener or any other man for that matter." As soon as the words left her lips, she regretted them. How could she snap at this man who had treated her with such respect and care? He was not Reginald, and he never would be. "Philip, I did not mean what I just said."

The wind blew the hair from his face as he gazed down at her. "You are only speaking the truth; your decisions are yours alone to make."

"It is not that," she said. "I have come to find my strength in you. Your wisdom has saved me numerous times already, and the thought of you not being there bothers me."

He turned his attention back to the ocean, but his words were kind and soothing as he said, "Wisdom can be learned, strength cannot. You have both, though you do not yet realize it. You will one day and I will be here to help where I can."

Her anger subsided and now confidence replaced it. No man had ever spoken such words to her nor made her feel so capable. And as they both watched the waves roll before them, she found that she liked his words more than ever.

***

The following days were busy with purchases of new dresses for Caroline, a new wardrobe for Oliver—the boy was growing out of everything he owned so quickly, she could barely keep up!—and, although he kept refusing, several new coats and breeches for Philip.

The seamstress had been adamant that the clothing for Caroline would be ready by tomorrow morning, although the time was short, and the tailor had also worked diligently to have the clothing for Oliver and Philip ready to be delivered the same day—all so they could begin the long journey home.

Caroline would have preferred to remain in Cornwall; the peacefulness of the oceanside and lack of responsibilities was what she had needed. Life could not be ignored, not if she wished to have an estate left for her son to run when he became of age.

Sporting a new hat on his head, Oliver walked beside his governess, as proud as a peacock. Caroline had never seen him in such a state; yet, he wore the first hat he had a hand in choosing. Granted, it was beyond his years in style, but he had been quite proud of choosing something that matched a choice Philip had made.

Caroline sneaked a glance at Philip through her lashes, who strolled beside her. He was the same stoic man he always was, and he seemed to take his position as protector very seriously as his eyes roved around as if in search of assassins.

Despite that stoicism, he was a handsome man. Yet, he still had shared nothing of his life with her. Who was he really? He did the work of a servant but spoke like nobility; that was not something one would expect of a servant. His mannerisms also belied his station. What secrets did this man hold?

"You realize that your hat does not hide your glances toward me, do you not?" Philip said with a chuckle.

Caroline sniffed, although, inside she held mirth. "Do not assume I was looking at you," she said with a jut to her chin, "for I was not."

He raised an eyebrow at her, and she could not hold in her laughter any longer. "Oh, very well! I was looking at you, but it is not what you believe."

His eyebrow raised further. "And what do I believe?"

Caroline almost tripped on a stone. "I-I am unsure what you believe, to be honest. You are very quiet."

"I am always quiet."

To this she gave a nod. The man was fascinating, that much was true. If only she could hear his thoughts or get him to speak about himself so she could know him better.

Then an idea came to her. Margaret had said that one way to loosen the tongue of a man was to ply him with drinks. Perhaps during dinner this evening she could get him to agree to several drinks with her.

She would, of course, stick to wine, for spirits could easily turn against her. She would see that he had several glasses of brandy or whiskey and see where that led.

Suddenly, Miss Lindston yelped and would have fallen if Philip had not raced forward and caught her by the arm.

"Are you all right?" he asked her.

"I believe so, Mr. Butler," she replied. "I'm afraid I was not watching where I was going." She smiled at him. "Thank you."

He returned her smile, and a burning in Caroline's stomach unsettled her. She placed her hand on her stomach and turned to a shop window, and she gazed through it without seeing what was inside. Had she eaten food that had disagreed with her? The prunes at the morning meal had seemed off.

She pushed aside the uneasiness and returned her thoughts to the matter at hand. She really did need to learn more about this man to whom she had entrusted her life and the life of her son.

"Your Grace," Miss Lindston said from behind her, "should I take Master Hayward back to the room for a nap?"

"No!" shouted Oliver as he rubbed his eyes. "I don't want to go to sleep."

"Now, Oliver, even if we are on holidays, your sleep is very important. Why do you not go on now and if you are good, I will allow you one small cake before bed. If not, you will get none. What say you?"

The young boy's stance changed. "Oh, yes, that would be nice," he said. Then he grabbed the governess's hand. "Come on, Miss Lindston. We have a cake to eat."

Caroline laughed at the urgency with which her son now spoke, but that laughter died when she noticed the smile the young governess gave Philip. "And Miss Lindston," she said before the pair could leave, "if you would please see that he is read a story? I am afraid I will be involved in some matters of business and will not be able to do so."

The woman gave her a curtsy and replied, "Of course, Your Grace."

As the pair walked away, Caroline stiffened her resolve. She had no business to which to attend;, yet if she wished to become closer to Philip, she had to strike quickly, or another woman would catch his eye.

How strange, she thought. She had seen Philip as handsome, to be sure, but until she had seen the look the governess had given him, she had not realized that she desired more from him that his protection. She desired more, indeed.

***

The sound of the waves crashing on the beach was relaxing, the full moon breathtaking, and the presence of Philip beside Caroline was spellbinding as they walked along the beach. Her plan to ply him with drinks had gone awry, for she suspected she was now more inebriated than he was. Rather than loosening his tongue, it was she who did most of the talking, but somehow she could not dam the flow of words.

"No one is about," she said in a chastising tone. "Why not pull back your hair." Did her words sound slurred?

"As you wish," he said, and he pulled back his hair over his shoulder.

Oh, yes, this man was handsome, exceedingly so, and she found she could not take her eyes off his face. What captured her was his smile; it was comforting and had a kindness to it, despite his reluctance to speak about himself.

"Thank you," he said, though he did not look at her. "I have been told I am handsome, but handsomeness does not define a man."

She stopped and stared at him aghast. Had she spoken aloud? But of course, she must have. Why had she consumed so much wine, and on such an important night of all times? How was she to glean any information from the man if she could not hold her wits about her?

Despite the horror she felt within, she could not stop the giggle from escaping her lips. Oh, really! She needed to pull herself together or all would be lost.

"This week has been a joy to Oliver and me," she said in an attempt to guide the conversation away from her bungle. "Even Miss Lindston has seemed to enjoy herself, courtesy of you."

"Oh?" he asked, still not looking at her. "And how is that? I have hardly spoken two words to the woman."

Caroline could not stop the snort she gave. "When you saved her from falling, I saw the look in her eyes. It was a look of a woman with specific interests in mind. You did not release your grip from her at first. Perhaps you enjoyed holding her."

What am I doing? Caroline thought frantically. *This deceitful tongue of mine!*

Philip stopped and turned to smile at her. "That could be true," he said, a bit of mischief dancing in his eyes. "Or perhaps I wanted to assure myself she was safe before I released her."

Caroline laughed. "Allow me to show you," she said, though inside she screamed, *No!* "Catch me."

With that, she fell forward and was relieved when Philip caught her, his strong arms holding her up at her waist. "Now, do not let go, and I shall act the part of Miss Lindston."

He gave her an amused smile and nodded.

"Oh, Philip," she said in that damsel-in-distress manner of the theater, her eyelashes batting dramatically, "thank you for saving me!" She giggled.

What a silly thing to do! her mind screamed. Yet she could not stop herself; her heart was in charge, fighting her mind for control of her tongue. "You are such a strong and handsome man. I can see why you are not letting go of me."

"If I let go," Philip said, his smile still filled with mirth, "Her Grace would dismiss me for allowing her governess to fall and be injured. It is for that reason I continue to hold you."

They stood there for several moments looking into each other's eyes, and Caroline could hardly breathe. The air around them had changed, as had the hold that Philip had on her. No longer was it keeping her from falling; now it held her close. "And why do you hold me now?" she asked. "Because I might dismiss you?"

He shook his head. "No. I still hold you because I do not want to see you hurt."

Nothing could have made her heart soar more than those words at that moment. "It was the same when you gave me water when you should not have; you risked your position so I would not suffer. I know that, in your arms, I could never suffer."

The last came out in a whisper, and her mind no longer chastised her words, for it had joined her heart, giving her the feeling of flight.

He went to speak, but she stood on her toes and pressed her lips to his. Although it was the first time she had kissed a man of her own free will, his response brought her back down to earth, for his lips did not press back. What she had expected was a reflection of what was in her heart, but instead, there was nothing.

"Why do you reject me?" she asked as she took a step back from him. "Am I not pretty enough for you?"

He offered her a smile that left her disappointed. What she should have seen was anguish or hurt, not this affable smile he wore. "I value our friendship all too much," he replied. "I do not wish to lose such a gift."

Anger coursed through her, although she knew deep inside that it lacked reason. She had opened herself up to him, and he dared to speak of *friendship*? "You told me we could not be friends, for if we became as such, you would have to leave me. Now I am in your arms and you reject me?" She knew she was shouting, but she could not stifle the words, her ire was so great. "Tell me, am I not suitable for you?" She brushed away the hot tears she could not keep from sliding down her cheeks. How could she have humiliated herself this way?

He remained calm in the wake of her anger. "You are far better than to be suitable for the likes of a man such as myself," he said in quiet contrast to her shouted words. "You have a sharp mind, a kind heart, and your beauty radiates upon a thousand hills."

"I do not understand! Why do you reject me?" she asked, unable to control the pleading in her voice. "Is there another?"

Then realization came to her as she saw the truth in his eyes. He loved someone, and that someone was not her. She had thrown herself at a man about whom she knew nothing. That had been the goal of this evening; to learn more about him. Instead, she had acted no better than Miss French.

"No need to explain," she said with a low voice. "I have embarrassed myself enough for a lifetime."

She turned to leave, but he reached out and grabbed her arm.

"No," he said. "You do not understand." How could his voice remain calm while hers was that of a raving madwoman? And from where had that madwoman come? Had she been hiding away inside her all this time, or had she conjured some angry spirit with her actions?

Despite from where these new emotions came, when she looked into his eyes and saw the pain within, she discovered she could not walk away. Not without hearing what he had to say.

"I once loved a woman," he said as he looked out across the waters. "I loved her more than anything in this world. Her death is a shame I carry to this day…and the reason I cannot love another."

The pain in his eyes deepened, and Caroline realized that she had misread him. She could have attributed it to the alcohol she had consumed, but she knew it was her own misguided naivety that was to blame. The alcohol had only brought forth what was inside. How she wished she could remove that pain he carried, but it could not be so, for the love about which she had wondered, he had experienced, and the loss of it had crushed him.

"I am sorry, Philip. I did not know."

He nodded, and they stood on that beach for several moments in silence, both lost in their own thoughts.

After some time, he turned and smiled down at her. "It is time I took on a friend, Caroline," he said. "I believe you are the finest friend a man or woman could ever want. If it is not too presumptuous of me, might I be your friend as well as your protector? Allow me this one honor and I will ask for nothing more."

She did not need to take time to consider his request. "I would like that," she replied. Then she surprised herself by wrapping her arms around him, not in the embrace of lovers but rather that of friendship. Although she would not have the love she had sought, she knew it was a special kind of fondness. For that she was happy and would cherish it always.

"You will always be my friend, Philip," she said. "And as my friend, you may never leave me, do you understand? Whether I marry one day or not."

He gave her a nod. "I understand," he said, and she believed him wholeheartedly.

Chapter Nine

Caroline watched from the window of what had once been the office Reginald had used when he wished to work without any distractions, which was often. Philip and Oliver walked down the garden path, Philip teaching him the names of the different flowers and plants as they strolled along. Oliver had taken an immediate enjoyment to learning about what grew in his garden, and Caroline found nothing wrong with such lessons. He was now the duke, but that did not mean he could not learn about that which many in his position would deem as beneath them, for all knowledge would only make the boy a stronger man.

She found it intriguing that only a few months ago, Caroline thought her future bleak, one from which she wished to run away. Her life had been misery, lacking in love, her son withheld from her. Now, the future was hers.

The day following her drunken expression of love, she had woken to a piercing headache and a shame from which she worried she would never find relief. Despite his rejection of her love, he had reached out to her in friendship, and for that she was glad. It was a beautiful friendship, and although deep in her heart she wished for more, she knew it was not meant to be.

Perhaps, in time, it could become more—when the man had healed properly from his loss—and she would be there waiting for him. For herself, there would be no other man, for in her heart, there was only Philip; he could deny that truth all he wanted, but she did not.

What she felt was not love in spite of her words that evening; she was not prepared to name it so now that she was in her right mind, for, in truth, she did not know what such a feeling was. Nor could she imagine holding onto such a feeling if it was not returned. For the time being, she would call the feeling beautiful, for that was what it was.

"With your promise to never leave me," she whispered, "I will wait forever."

How a woman such as herself came from the poorest of homes to be where she was today still amazed her. With all that she possessed and the wealth at her disposal, she could have whatever came to mind, could purchase whatever her heart wanted, yet she had no desire to do so. What she wished for above all else was time with her son; therefore, what time she had with Philip was wonderful but not necessarily the most important.

"Your Grace," Quinton said from the doorway with a worried look. "You have callers; though, they refuse to enter." He had always been a man of unflappable character, but the arrival of these guests had clearly unsettled him.

"Who are they?" she asked.

Quinton refused to look at her, which only piqued her curiosity all the more.

"Come now," she said as she turned toward him. "I cannot imagine who would come calling that would leave you speechless."

The butler cleared his throat and said, "It is Lord Hayward and Miss French."

He had been right to be hesitant in introducing Reginald's brother and mistress. The entire household knew of Neil's treacherousness, or they had to, and as to Miss French, well, it had been clear to everyone where she stood when Reginald was alive.

Anger coursed through her as she straightened her back and walked as regally as she could past Quinton toward the front door. She had told both in no uncertain terms that they were not welcome in the house any longer, and yet, here they were, at her door? Well, she would see them thrown into prison for trespass if she had anything to do with it.

When she opened the door, she stood shocked as she looked upon a woman who resembled Miss French only in her features. She now wore a dress made of burlap, not much different from the one Caroline herself had been forced to wear during her day working in the gardens.

Beside her stood Neil. The man lacked his usual arrogance, and Caroline could not help but be suspicious.

It was not only those two who stood on the stoop. Beside Neil stood a tall man with handsome features and impeccable clothing. He looked to be around the age of thirty, his hair yet possessing any signs of gray, but the smallest of lines shown in the corners of his eyes.

"Your Grace," the man said with a diffident bow, "I am Lord Franklin Mullens, Baron of Routerly, and I wish to speak to you about a concerning matter that includes yourself."

"I am afraid I do not understand," Caroline said, wishing all three would leave. "Neil…?"

"I know you said never to return, but I believe you will find my disobedience worthwhile," Neil replied. "Nevertheless, if you wish me to leave, I will do so."

How strange to have this man treating her with such respect. Not once during her five years of marriage had the man ever shown any sign of deference. His actions made her suspicious while at the same time curious.

"No, stay," she relented. She would hear them out and if she did not like what they had to say, they would be thrown out on their ears. "Please, come inside. There is no reason for us to stand here when we have a perfectly good sitting room inside."

Caroline led the trio down the hall and into the sitting room. Once she had taken her place on the sofa and the men in two of the chairs, she was pleased when Miss French remained standing, her head bowed and her hands clasped in front of her. Caroline did not bother to offer any tea; they would not be staying long if she had anything to do with it.

When everyone was situated, Lord Mullens continued. "Your Grace, I believe that Miss French has something to say to you."

Caroline turned expectantly to her husband's mistress but said nothing, for she had nothing to say to the woman.

Much to Caroline's surprise, the woman gave her an unpracticed curtsy and said, "Your Grace, I sought after what was not mine, and my actions might never be forgiven." Her words sounded practiced. "I know I can't ever earn your favor, but I want you to know how sorry I am for what I've done, and I ask your forgiveness so I can begin a new life as a better person."

Caroline knew her snort was unladylike, but she did not care. "And how do you plan to do that?"

Neil answered for the woman. "She will work at my estate, knowing what it is like to earn an honest wage. She humiliated not only herself but you, as well, and I will see that she pays for what she has done."

With a thoughtful gaze, Caroline looked at the woman, her anger now replaced by pity. She had every reason to return the woman's disrespect with cruelty, to scream at her, and even strike her. Yet revenge was a foreign idea to Caroline. Furthermore, she had been on the receiving end of such harsh treatment. Would doing the same be hypocritical of her? No, she would not do those things, for kindness was the only action she could take.

"Very well," she replied. "I hope you find peace."

"Your kindness precedes you," Lord Mullens said.

Caroline acknowledged the compliment, but her mind was on other things. She walked over and pulled the ring chord. When Quinton appeared, she said, "See that Lord Mullens is served tea." Then she turned to Neil. "I will speak to you alone, if you please."

Neil rose and bowed. "Of course, Your Grace," he said. "Mary, you will wait out in the carriage."

Miss French curtsied without lifting her eyes. "Yes, My Lord," she said and then made her way outside. Caroline had to stop herself from gaping after the woman.

Neil bowed once more to Caroline. "After you, Your Grace."

His words sounded flat to Caroline, yet she was not the person her husband had been, one who found only the bad in people. No, she was better than he, and this was how she would prove it.

***

Once the door to the office was closed, Caroline turned back to Neil, and though he smiled, she did not return it. Two months earlier the man had put his hands on her, had tried to force a kiss upon her. Although she had done nothing to influence the man, she had been left humiliated and with a feeling of defilement, and she refused to be forced to feel that way again.

"What is it you want?" she demanded before he was able to speak. She offered him no seat and he did not request one. "Who is that man and how do you know him?"

"If I may tell you a story," he said, "then perhaps you will understand." Was that humility she heard? It could not be, for the man did not know the meaning of humble.

"If you must," she said in a curt tone.

He sighed. "There was once a boy who grew up in the shadow of his brother. This boy mimicked every move his brother made, for the brother had everything the boy ever wanted. In the process, that boy grew to be a cold, twisted man, overcome with lust for money."

Caroline raised an eyebrow at him. If he expected sympathy, the man would be waiting for a very long time for it.

"It was when the older brother died that the younger thought to gain both title and wealth for himself. As days passed, he began to think. For forty of his fifty years he had sought wealth and land, yet he was not happy. He soon began to realize all the wrong he had done in his life, and he felt sick from it."

"And what does this have to do with me?" Caroline asked, not believing a man could change so much in such a short amount of time. "And what of this Lord Mullens?"

"Mullens had come to settle some business affairs with me, affairs that included both Reginald and myself. When he learned what his sister had been up to…"

"His sister?" Caroline asked, mortified.

"Indeed. Mary French, or so she had come to call herself, is actually Miss Mary Mullens."

Caroline grimaced. The woman was the sister of a baron? How humiliating that had to be for poor Lord Mullens to learn that his sister had been mistress to a duke. "Go on," she said, smoothing her face once more.

"As you can imagine, he was irate when he learned how his sister had been behaving. When he spoke to me about it, I realized that I felt shame, as well. Shame for standing by and watching it happen, for encouraging it, and for remaining silent. Lord Mullens is twenty years my younger but has shown to be far wiser than I." He sighed. "I say all this to express two things. First, I want to apologize for my actions and words toward you over the years you were married to my brother; they were reprehensible."

A frost in her veins began to melt, and she began to see this man in a different light. Did not everyone deserve a second chance?

"I forgive you," she said. Forgiveness did not mean she would forget, but that she kept to herself.

He released held breath. "Thank you," he whispered. "The second thing I wish to say is this. With Reginald now gone and with no children of my own, Oliver is all I have left. I will never set foot in your house again, but grant me once a fortnight to come and see him. If only for a few minutes." The man lowered his head as if in that diffidence that seemed so strange on him.

Caroline could only stand in shock. Could this man have changed so drastically? She had already forgiven him his transgressions. Was she ready to allow him to influence Oliver, as well? How she wished Philip was by her side, for he would know how to guide her.

She walked over to the window and watched Philip and Oliver, their heads together as they peered down at a budding daisy. She could ask him to come inside, but did she not need to make her own decisions? She was the Dowager Duchess, and she was in charge of her son's upbringing. What did she know of being a man with a title and the responsibilities that went with that station? Indeed, what did Philip know of such things?

Glancing over at Neil, she made a decision. "You may come by and see him, but know that I will be close by. Trust is earned, never given."

Neil raised his head and smiled broadly. "Thank you," he said. "I will wait in the carriage for Lord Mullens." He gave her another deep bow, this one deserving of a member of the royal family, and went to walk out the door.

Letting out a sigh, Caroline called him back. "Neil, wait," she said, hoping she was not making a huge mistake. "Please, join us in the sitting room."

Chapter Ten

Tea had been served, and the conversation was pleasant enough; although Caroline could not shake the strange feeling of being in the presence of a Neil Hayward who was quiet and attentive. Yet, it was not only his silence she found unsettling but the way he seemed to absorb every word Lord Mullens had to say.

"Once Neil informed me that my holdings were now split between himself and you," Lord Mullens was saying, "I must admit that the idea excited me."

"How so?" Caroline asked carefully as she hid her suspicions behind the teacup she brought to her lips.

"To be perfectly honest, I have never done business with a woman before, much less a duchess. It is an honor of which I had heard but have never thought I would ever experience."

Neil snorted. "Women have no head for business," he said. "It is not the way nor will it ever be. Why would anyone believe that it would?" Then his eyes went wide as he looked at Caroline. "I mean…that is…besides you, of course."

Caroline suppressed a laugh. There was the man that lived behind that face. "Of course."

Lord Mullens smiled at her. "You are right, Neil. It has not been the way of things. Yet, those ways are changing, are they not? I have seen more women open their own businesses—millineries and such—and they are quite successful. It is imperative that we men change with them, for if we do not, I fear a lady such as the Dowager Duchess here will be ruling over us all and we will end up working for her!"

Caroline did laugh at this. Although she had only known the man for an hour, she found his company more than enjoyable. A man with title and wealth who was still kind? She would never have believed it if she had not seen it for herself.

Neil sighed. "I suppose you are right. Still, I do not understand it all."

"You will learn soon enough, my friend," Lord Mullens said as he stood. "Now, shall we leave the duchess alone or continue to bore her with our stories?"

Caroline set her teacup aside and stood. She was surprised that she was sad to see Lord Mullens leave. "Oh, you are not boring me at all," she said. "I find your stories fascinating. I do look forward to doing business with you in the future."

Neil shook his head as he made his way to the door, but Caroline ignored him. It took much for a tiger to change his stripes.

Lord Mullens leaned in and lowered his voice. "Give him time," he whispered. "His stubbornness is great, but he is making progress."

Caroline smiled. "I will," she promised, and found she meant it. "Perhaps it is time to bury the hatchet, as they say."

"Indeed," the man replied. "If I may be so bold. When I come to collect Mary in two weeks' time from your brother-in-law's home, may I call on you so we might continue our conversation?"

A wave of thoughts rushed through her, tumbling one over the other at once, causing her head to pound. Fear set upon her in reaction to the manner in which Reginald had treated her whenever she spoke to another man. Yet, her husband was no longer alive to chastise or punish her. Furthermore, the man calling upon her for conversation was in no way a wrongdoing.

Then there was her concern for Philip. She could not risk falling for another man while she had promised to wait for him. Then again, this man was not asking to court her but rather to simply call by and have conversation with her. What was the harm in that?

Her hesitation must have seeped through, for Lord Mullens said, "I forget my place. I should not have been so forward. It has been an honor to make your acquaintance." He gave her a low bow and clapped Neil on the back. "Come, my friend, we have much to discuss about the future."

With a relieved smile, Caroline walked the two men to the door. When they were gone, she shut the door and let out a sigh. Lord Mullens had mentioned the future and women being a part of it, and she found an excitement at the idea.

Yet, although she knew she would have a happy future no matter what path she took, the only way it could be complete was if Philip was by her side. She could not have denied that if she tried.

***

Caroline sat alone in her rooms, rooms that had once belonged to the duke himself. He had taken the most opulent rooms for himself, of course, leaving Caroline with a tiny room in the attic. Once, he had shared these with her, but only until she conceived. Then she was sent away.

She was not one to wish for more than she had. Life had been difficult when she was young; her parents struggled to make ends meet and to put food on the table. They at least loved her. Sharing a room with four other siblings had been a challenge, to say the least, but she would have given everything to return to those days after what she had endured once she was wed.

Now, the largest rooms were hers, and despite the pettiness of her pleasure in having what Reginald had once denied her, she did enjoy them. The bed had been replaced—she would not sleep upon a bed her husband had shared with another woman—as had the heavy oak drawers and wardrobe. Instead, she had purchased all new furniture that suited her far better than the masculine and oppressive pieces the duke had utilized.

A sound in the small sitting room that led to the hallway made her turn. Then there was a light tap on the frame of the door she had left open.

"Caroline?" Philip called from the other room. "You sent for me?"

"I did," she replied. "Come here. I want to show you something."

The man peeked into the bedroom, clearly uncomfortable with entering her bedchamber, which amused her greatly. He was her protector! What if she was set upon by someone in this very room? Would she die because of his disquiet?

"What is it?" he asked as he came to stand beside her at the window.

He was tense in his dark blue tailcoat and tan trousers, and she wondered if his discomfort came from being in her room or from wearing clothes with which he was unaccustomed. The clothing did not appear strange on him as it might on another servant given clothes they were not used to wearing. He wore his new attire with aplomb.

"Do you remember what happened down there only a few months ago?" she asked.

He glanced out the window. "I do. You were pulling weeds from the garden, tilling the soil with your hands. Suffering for sins you did not commit."

"Yes," Caroline replied with a sigh. "As I toiled, tearing my hands, I looked up to this very window. Miss French—or should I say Miss Mullens—sneered down at me. Then Reginald was kissing her before leading her away from the window, presumably to his bed."

Philip remained quiet, for which Caroline was relieved.

"I often thought about what I would say to the woman if I ever saw her again," Caroline continued. "What I would say to her. What I would do to her. None of it was congenial. I thought that doing so would bring about relief and therefore ease the pain of that day. Once given the chance, I found I could not do those horrid things. What I felt for the woman when I saw her today was pity." She turned her gaze toward Philip. "Then, my husband's brother, a man who treated me with utter disrespect and such brashness I had him thrown out of my house, he requests to spend time with my son. And I agree! Am I a fool?"

Philip gazed down at her. "You are no fool," he replied. "You are a kind woman with a good heart and mind. What you went through for all those years still lingers inside you; the pain is still evident."

Caroline nodded her agreement. Releasing her hurt and anger was not an easy task, and she still suffered bouts of anxiety and fear. She had become stronger, and she attributed that to the man beside her.

"As to Miss French," he continued, "the woman was in the wrong; there is no doubt about that. Let her go her own way, for her path is twisted. You must find your happiness from within, not in the actions of others."

She smiled at him. "How is it that my protector is so wise?" she asked.

"You are wise, but you doubt yourself."

His words were sensible, and he was correct in what he said. Yet she could not shake that doubt of which he spoke.

"And what of Neil?" she asked. "I cannot help but think that he is still scheming in some way. He tried to kiss me not two months ago. Now, he pleads ignorance and a desire to change his ways?" She let out a sigh. "I am unsure as to what to do."

Her mind and soul were filled with a heavy foreboding she could not shake. Every time she thought of Neil, she then thought of Reginald. He would have been infuriated with the situation, and somehow he still held onto a small part of her deep inside. Too often, she could hear him screaming at her from the other side of the door, flinging insults at her and belittling her.

But no. He was dead and buried, and she had to release the ghost that held over her that bit of fear. If she did not, she truly would go mad.

Then Philip placed a hand on her arm, and all the fear, all the anxiety, disappeared. It was as if he had magic in his being, a magic that wiped away everything bad and replaced it with good.

"You are wise to keep him close," Philip said. "For you will be able to determine if his intentions are pure. Follow your instincts and your heart and allow them to guide you. For when the heart leads, only goodness can follow. That which is not good shall be cast aside."

Caroline smiled. His words were as comforting as his touch, and she wished to embrace him, to have him hold her. Yet, she knew that could not happen, not now, anyway. But one day, he would be healed from his own pain, just as she would be healed from hers, and until then, she would accept his wise counsel and allow her heart to guide her. Good things, such as Philip, would remain.

Chapter Eleven

Philip looked down over the gardens from the library window, watching as Neil walked beside Oliver. The man had been by twice to see the boy over the past month, and Philip could not have been more pleased. For without the man, his plans would have been forfeit.

When the duke had died, Philip had lamented. Not for the man's death, of course, for the man was cruel and heartless in every way, but rather for the dissolution of the scheme he had mapped out much too carefully. Then, when Caroline had pushed Neil away, as well, he thought all had been lost.

He had spent too much time crafting his plan to change course now, which began with gaining employment at Blackwood Estates and finding his place amongst the servants. He had to observe from afar, thus why he had not attempted to work within the house. Too much could be seen, much he wished to keep hidden, if he had remained so close.

It was not difficult to allow his imagination to go off gallivanting on its own, for once his plan was executed, Philip would finally find peace in the destruction he had caused. An old grievance would be made right, and he would be free to move on with his life. The deception he had to use was regretful, but it was also necessary.

He smiled as he heard movement behind him. "Although your footsteps have become quieter," he said without turning, "your breathing gives you away, as do your skirts."

Caroline laughed and came to stand at his side.

"Will I ever be able to take you by surprise?" she asked with amusement.

He turned to her. His eyes had never lied to him, and therefore there was no doubt that the woman who stood before him was a beautiful creature. Her hair had been pinned back, tiny curls left to ring her heart-shaped face. He tried to ignore how her dress accentuated her slim waist and ample bosom, and he had to force back the desire to pull her into his arms and kiss her—forever if he could.

That would have to wait for now; for after his plan was complete. Too much was at stake to gamble for a single kiss, no matter how extraordinary it might have been.

"Perhaps one day you will," he said, pushing the huskiness from his voice. He turned back to look out the window, if only to keep from looking at her any longer than was necessary. "The two seem happy together," he said with a lift of his chin to indicate he spoke of Neil and Oliver.

"Yes, they do," she replied. "Neil truly has changed since Reginald's passing, and I believe his influence over the boy will be good." She turned toward him. "He has invited Oliver and me to dinner in a week's time, though I wonder if it is moving too quickly. Although he has shown he has changed, I cannot calm that tiny ball of fear that still resides inside me."

"I believe you should go," Philip replied, though he cringed when he realized he had blurted out the words.

"I have never seen you so enthusiastic," Caroline teased. "Tell me, why do you wish me to go? Do you want to see me away from home…and away from you?" She looked up at him through her lashes, and if he did not know her as well as he did, he would have suspected that she was flirting with him. That could not be so, for they had decided, together, that they would remain only friends.

"Not at all," he said, doing his best to rectify the situation. "It will be good to mend old ties, and I have always wanted to see his estate."

She narrowed her eyes at him. "Oh, you assume you will be going with us? Has my protector now taken over my scheduling?"

His heart raced. Had he overstepped? Would everything now be lost because he had been hasty and had spoken out of turn? But no. The smile on her lips belied the severe tone of her words.

He relaxed and replied, "I cannot lie. That is my plan."

She laughed, that glorious set of dancing crystals on a chime. Then she said, "Very well, then. I will tell Neil that we accept."

Philip smiled as he pulled his hair over his shoulder. He had to tread very carefully here. "Please understand that I will go as your protector. I do not expect, nor would I feel comfortable with dining with you and your former brother-in-law. It would not be appropriate to have a servant at the table." When she gave him a concerned look, he added, "Do not worry; I will be close by if any danger comes, but it is important that family sits together."

She tilted her head in thought for a moment and then nodded. "You are right," she agreed. "Although, I must admit that I have grown accustomed to having you dine with us. You will be missed."

"Have no doubt that I will miss you, too," he said, and without thinking, he reached out and took her hand in his. Her skin was soft and warm, gentle compared to his own, and he let it go rather than fight down those feelings of desire once again.

He forced his gaze to return to the window. "I suppose you will want to speak with Neil," he said. "I have things to which I should attend, as well." He gave her a bow and left the room before she could stop him.

Once in the hallway, he paused and closed his eyes for a moment. His heart was pulling him in two different directions, causing him grief. Although he wished only to return to the woman in that room, he pushed it aside. He had a mission to complete—and a letter to write—and that had to take precedence above everything else. Including his heart.

***

After so much planning and patience, Philip was finally inside the home of Lord Neil Hayward, and he could not have been more pleased. The home was large, as would be befitting of the brother of a duke, but Philip was disappointed at the drabness of the place. Few paintings hung from the walls, and the curtains on the windows had not been drawn back fully. The décor lacked color and was as flat as the man who owned it. Yet, none of that mattered; what lay beyond did.

"Well," Neil said with a wide smile, "shall we head to the dining room?" He placed a hand on Oliver's shoulder and smiled down at him. "I would guess you are hungry?" When he glanced up at Philip, that smile disappeared. "The servants' hall is through that door behind you. Food will be brought to you shortly."

Philip gave him a stiff bow. He had pulled his hair back and tied it with a ribbon but allowed it to still cover the sides of his face. Showing his face still did not make him comfortable, but he had promised Caroline that he would meet her halfway. Whether or not Neil approved made no difference to Philip, but he could tell the man did not. Rather than allowing anger to take over, he let Neil's disapproval slide off him like rain on a cloak.

"Thank you, My Lord," Philip said. "Er...may I beg a favor of you? I forgot my book in my room back at Blackwood Estates. Would it be possible to peruse your library so I might have something to read? I would not ask, but it will keep me occupied while I wait." He looked to Caroline, hoping she would intervene and hid a smile when she did.

"That would be fine, do you not think, Neil?"

The man gave a half-snort. "My office is in there. Please wait until after you eat; I do not want my books ruined with food dropped by your careless fingers." Without another word, the man turned and offered his arm to Caroline.

Caroline gave Philip a small smile and then placed her hand on the arm of her host. They walked down the hallway, Oliver falling close behind.

Philip shook his head and then headed through the door Neil had indicated. There he found a long table, probably used by the house servants for meals, with one place setting.

A footman was setting a bowl with steam rising from its contents, and Philip could smell the hearty aroma of stew. Beside the bowl, the man placed a plate with hunks of bread on it.

"Thank you," Philip said to the footman. He pulled out the chair and sat. In the next room, he could hear the clatter of kitchenware and was pleased that no one seemed to pay him any mind beyond seeing that he had received his food.

He was not hungry, but to not eat would arouse suspicion that he did not want. Therefore, as he consumed his meal, he allowed himself a few moments to think about how he had arrived at this point in his life.

The scheme had seemed so simple, but implementation had proven much more difficult than he had anticipated. Upon arrival at Blackwood Estates less than a year earlier, the duke had rejected his offer to replace his gardener.

Philip had no references; therefore, he had no proof that he had experience. When he offered to do the work for significantly less than the going rate, the duke had accepted. Then, once in position, Philip had allowed himself to move to the background, to blend into his surroundings. Soon, no one noticed him; only the work he had completed with surprising competence.

What he had not anticipated was how he would react when he laid eyes on Caroline. Her beauty and heart had captivated him at that very moment, and he found that he had grown fond of her. He had to keep a strict discipline of not allowing his emotions to guide him. As luck would have it, he had better sensibilities than that. Or at least he hoped he did. It was certainly a struggle.

He looked down, surprised that he had finished off all the stew. He pushed the bowl away. There was no time to dwell on the past; only the future was important now, as he was fond of telling Caroline. His future resided in an office down the hallway, and he rose and thanked the cook, who gave him a wave and a smile.

The office was easy to find, and he was thankful that sunlight still peeked through the curtains. He walked over to a bookshelf containing a line of brown and blue ledgers. At the least, he had an hour to search for the information he needed, and he pulled one of the books from the shelf and set about perusing through the notations in search of one particular piece of information that would confirm his suspicions. He did not find what he needed. Disappointed, he returned the ledger to its place and pulled out the next, repeating the process many times. He could not have been wrong!

As the hour neared and precious light began to fade, he slammed close the cover of the ledger before him in frustration.

"Think!" he whispered. The sum for which he searched was great, and the Haywards were much too meticulous to not have noted it. He had no doubt it was here. Somewhere.

Philip placed his head in his hands, and a pen fell to the floor. As he bent to pick it up, he noticed another ledger hidden on the bottom shelf. He picked up the book and set it on the desk, returning the one he had been looking through back on the shelf so he would not forget it later.

As he looked down at the well-worn black cover, his heart began to race. This had to be it; this had to be the one for which he had been searching. He opened the book and ran his fingers down the page, until finally, his eyes fell on a set of notations. The sum had been logged and then divided, half sent to a company he did not recognize but a name he would never forget. He wanted to scream for joy as he replaced the ledger where he had found it.

When he turned, his breath caught in his throat.

"What do you find so interesting?" Miss Mary Mullens asked with a smile. She wore an emerald-green gown, her hair in a perfect coiffure. Apparently, her servant days were behind her and she had assumed some role of importance in the house.

"I find many of the books on these shelves intriguing," he said, cursing himself inwardly for not hearing her approach.

Her eyes looked past him, and she stepped closer, her bosom pressing against his arm, her face tilted up. "I find it hard to believe that you do not know the difference between a book that can be read and a ledger," she said, her smile more a sneer. "Though, I also find it hard to believe a simple gardener can read." She placed a hand on his chest, and he had to push back the revulsion that welled up inside him.

"Why do you hide behind your hair?" She reached up to push it back and he grabbed her arm.

"If you will excuse me," he said in a low voice. "I shall go wait in the kitchen."

He went to move past her, but she shifted, blocking his exit with a laugh. "Neil will be upset if I told him what I saw," she whispered in an overly sweet voice. "Though, perhaps we can come to an agreement that will make me change my mind." Her smile was seductive as her finger traced circles on his chest.

"What do you want?" he asked, angry for having put himself in this situation. Had he been more alert she would not have gained the upper hand. Yet, it was past time for regret, and if she called for Neil, all would be lost.

"I see the way the duchess looks at you, and I understand why. So, give me a single kiss now, and it will seal my lips."

He scrunched his brow. What game was this? What man in his right mind would believe a woman such as this to keep her tongue quiet simply by giving her a kiss?

She shrugged. "Very well," she said and turned to leave.

With no choice, he reached out and grabbed her arm. As much as he hated to do it, he could not allow this woman to expose him. Therefore, he leaned over and touched his lips to hers. She reached her arms around his neck and tried to pull him closer, but he pushed her away.

"You got your kiss," he said. "Now, let me by."

She smiled at him. "And it was a lovely kiss," she said. "Perhaps I can receive more at another time." Then she walked out of the room.

Philip shook his head, staring after her for a moment. Then he left the room, and the ledger, and returned to the servants' hall.

Chapter Twelve

Caroline stifled a giggle as she watched Neil interact with Oliver. The man had truly changed, and it warmed her heart to know good did exist in him. They had completed their meal, and a footman returned for the third time this evening to refill her wine glass. The drink was making her lightheaded, making her louder than she intended.

"I apologize for my laughter," she said as she covered her mouth with a hand. "I believe the wine is stronger than I anticipated."

Neil looked her way and smiled. "Please, there is no need for apologies. We all need laughter. Is that not right, Oliver?"

The boy nodded, a wide grin on his face. "Oh, yes," he replied. "I like to laugh."

"As do we all, Nephew," Neil said.

Caroline took another sip of her wine, happy that what had been broken before was now mended. Oliver needed his family, including his uncle, and it was only right that he get to know the man in a different light. In the past, Oliver had said he did not like the man, but now, his smile told a different story.

Now that Oliver was taken care of, she needed to turn her attention to Philip and the pain he carried. Although she knew the man would be resistant at first, she believed he would come around if she was able to show him how healing life could be.

"Would that be all right with you?"

Caroline started. "I am sorry," she said, shaking her head to clear away the thoughts—and the effects of the wine. "What was that?"

"I was speaking of my journey to France tomorrow. When Oliver is older, perhaps he will be able to accompany me."

Oliver's face was alight. "Oh, I would so enjoy such a journey!" he exclaimed. "Might I, Mother? I promise to behave for Uncle Neil."

Caroline chuckled. "Yes, when you are older, you may," she replied. "For now, you must continue with your studies. You have a great responsibility as the Duke of Browning, and you must be ready to assume those responsibilities when you are older."

Neil gave her an appreciative nod. "Your mother is right. You must study daily, and most importantly, listen to her, for she knows what is best for you."

The bolt of pride that struck Caroline was a surprise. This man, who had once been cruel and calculating, had become endearing. She would never have thought it possible if she had not seen it with her own eyes.

"I realize you must be leaving soon," Neil said, rising from his chair, "but there is something I wish to give you." He walked around to stand behind her and rested his hands on her shoulders.

The old fears returned, and she stiffened beneath the intimate touch. Had she misread the man? Was he back to his old ways, attempting to seduce her as he once had? She prayed all he had shown her was not an act.

"My mother raised Reginald and me with love and compassion," he said, "Our father was a brutal man who was strict and had a heart of stone. Mother was not strong enough to stop the man from twisting our minds, but she did what she could to see we learned something of love." He sighed heavily. "Nevertheless, when I was younger, she gave me a very special gift that I was to give to my wife. Seeing as I have never married, it is only fitting that such a lovely necklace go to a deserving woman. Would you not agree, Oliver?"

"Yes, Uncle," Oliver said with an emphatic nod.

Caroline did not look up at Neil. Her confusion, as well as her fear, froze her in place, and it was only when the man removed his hands from her shoulders that she relaxed at all.

He walked over to a small table where a box she had noticed before lay. When he returned, in his hands he held a necklace that was beautiful and appeared quite expensive. It displayed the largest sapphire she had ever seen, the light glinting off its perfect angles as it hung from a silver chain.

"This is for you," Neil said. Without asking, he returned to stand behind her, his fingertips grazing her skin as he placed the necklace around her neck, the blue pendant falling between her breasts. "Now, what do you think?" He adjusted the pendant, and Caroline found it difficult not to shrink back from his touch.

"It-it is beautiful," she managed to say, although her heart pounded in her chest. "But I cannot accept such a gift."

He gave her shoulders a gentle squeeze and then returned to his seat. "You must accept," he said. "I will not take no for an answer." He turned to Oliver. "Your first lesson, Oliver. Remember it well."

"I will," Oliver said with a smile.

Neil raised his glass. "To family. May we stay by each other through the best and worst of times."

Caroline forced a smile as she lifted her own glass. Had she read more into the manner in which the man had touched her? His attention had returned to Oliver, and he gave her not a second glance. Had those old fears attempted to ruin what was clearly a gracious gesture? As she watched the man once again interacting with Oliver, she realized that she had come close to doing just that.

After some time passed, filled with laughter and talk, the tall clock in the hall chimed. "It is getting late," she said, finding it strange she felt a bit of reluctance to leave. "I will have Philip see the carriage brought around. Oliver, behave yourself." She smiled down at him knowing full well he would.

As she walked past him, she fingered the pendant. It was a beautiful necklace, and what Neil had said was true. He had no wife of his own, so what better way to fulfill the wishes of his mother than to see the necklace remained in the family. She would not have been unhappy if his wife, if he had one, had received the piece, but the gesture had been touching. She could not wait to show it to Philip and hear his thoughts about it, for she thought a lot about his opinion.

She had to pass several rooms on her way to the foyer, and passing one that had its door open, she stopped in shock as Philip pull a woman into his arms and kissed her.

It was not the kiss itself that had set her heart to plummet to her feet, although the thought of him kissing another left her breathless. No, what sent her over the edge was the person who was on the receiving end of that kiss, for it was none other than the adulterous and treacherous woman who had been mistress to Reginald.

She placed her back against the wall in order to will her lungs to take in breath. As she stood there, the room reeling around her, Miss Mullens walked out of the room. Thankfully, the woman had not seen her, and Caroline pursed her lips, readying herself for her encounter with the man she had thought had been her supporter.

When Philip walked through the door, she had her emotions under control and she forced a smile.

"Are you ready?" she asked, startling the man.

"I am," he replied, returning her smile easily.

How the man had duped her! When her eyes had been focused on whether or not Neil would somehow weasel his way into her life, Philip had sneaked in from behind. Well, she would not allow him to get whatever it was that he wanted from her. What that was, she did not know, but she intended to find out.

***

Caroline nursed a glass of brandy, her third since they had returned home two hours earlier, as she stood on the veranda that looked over the gardens. The stars offered her little consolation, for she could only replay that dreaded moment when she saw Philip kiss Miss Mullens. How was it she could allow the man's actions to hurt her so? He was free to pursue whomever he chose, was he not? Many mysteries existed in the world, yet the one that bothered her at this moment was herself.

"You are still drinking I see," Philip said as he came to stand beside her.

Caroline studied the hair that covered his features. She should have seen it before in that simple stance; he hid everything from the everyone; therefore, why should it be any different for her?

"And if I am?" she asked in cool tones. "Do you care or is it you simply wish to mock me?"

He shifted his stance and looked down. "Of course I care," he said quietly.

She gave him a sniff. "I do not believe you," she said. She pulled her head back and emptied the glass in one go. Of course, it was an unladylike manner to do so, but the action gave her a feeling of satisfaction. He did not deserve to be treated as an equal. Was she not a duchess and he only a simple protector who had once been a gardener?

"I am sorry you believe so little of me," he said.

"You only care for yourself," she snapped. She grabbed the parapet to keep herself from falling. When he reached for her arm, she pulled away. "Leave me be," she hissed.

"If that is what you wish."

His voice carried such a sad note, she wondered, not for the first time, if she was being overly dramatic. But no, she had seen him pull *that woman* into his arms and kiss her. She had every reason to be angry with him! If it had been any other woman, she would not have taken it so badly.

Or would she have? Could she say with complete honesty she would have reacted in any other way if the woman had not been the former mistress of her now deceased husband? In all honesty, she could not. Granted, her anger might have been less heated, but it would have been there nonetheless. What she wished to do at that moment was pummel the man with her fist!

"I have upset you in some way," he said in that caring tone that mocked her heart. "Please, tell me what I have done to displease you."

Caroline studied him for a moment. Should she reveal what she had seen? Could she stand the lies he would be made to tell to mask the truth? She should not have consumed the amount of brandy she had, for it had muddled her thinking.

"Oh, it does not matter anymore," she said with a wave of her hand. "I have made a fool of myself in how I have dealt with you. I am a duchess; what business do I have giving chase after a man who is in my employ? It seems I am no better than my husband in that aspect."

He reached out for her once again, but the very last thing she wished was to feel his hand touching her. "You cannot compare yourself to your husband," he said. "And you have done nothing wrong."

Tears rolled down her cheeks unchecked. "Do not mock me any longer," she whispered. Why would she be crying? "You see me as some piece in a game, dangling my feelings in front of me."

"Caroline, I must admit I have no idea of what you speak. What is it that I have done to upset you so?"

Again, she wondered if sharing her thoughts would be the wisest of ideas. He would only use it against her later, would he not? No, she was tired of this conversation.

She wiped the tears from her face with a kerchief and then straightened her back. "Lord Mullens showed an interest in me," she said, hoping to change the direction of the conversation. "Do you believe I should allow him to call on me?"

"If that is what you wish."

Infuriating man! "You know what I wish," she snapped. "Now, answer me."

He sighed and clasped his hands behind his back. How did a gardener learn to stand so regally? "I do not," he replied.

"And why is that?"

"I do not believe his intentions are honorable, seeing the company he keeps."

"Liar!" she said. "Let me see your face."

He said nothing as he moved the hair back from his face, and what she saw confused her. What she had expected was to see pride etched in his features, yet what she found was pain.

"I do not lie," he said in that quiet, controlled voice. "I only wish to see you happy, and that man cannot be the one who will do so."

"If you are so concerned for my happiness," she said through clenched teeth, "then why did you kiss Miss Mullens? Of all the women you could have chosen, you chose her? Do you realize how much your actions have hurt me?"

It was quiet for a moment, the only sound the rustling of leaves in the trees. Then he spoke. "Sometimes what we see is not the complete story. Yes, I did as you say, but for reasons other than what you imply."

"'Reasons other than what I imply'?" she asked incredulously. "There are only two reasons a man kisses a woman: he either loves her or lusts for her. So, which is it for you?"

Philip said nothing for several moments, and Caroline worried he would leave. At that moment, she wished he would; it would make things that much easier. Later, when she was thinking lucidly once again, she knew she would regret it.

He let out a heavy sigh and turned toward her. "She was blackmailing me."

Caroline could not stop herself from gaping at the man. "Do you expect me to believe such a thing?"

"I cannot convince you of the truth," he replied. "But that is what it is."

She narrowed her eyes at him. "How?"

He returned his gaze to the gardens. "It does not matter."

The audacity of the man! Had he no respect for her station? "It matters quite a bit," she said. "Tell me the truth now, or you may leave and never return."

The expression his face assumed in reaction to her words pierced her heart. Yet she had to know the truth. She had endured abuse and lies during the past five years; she would not spend the remainder of her years on this Earth subjected to further acts such as these.

At first, she worried he would not respond, that he would call her bluff and leave her. He placed a hand on the parapet and said, "I was looking through the ledgers in Neil's office, wondering about his transactions. She caught me and threatened to tell him if I did not kiss her. So, rather than being exposed for my prying, I granted her that which she requested. When she had what she wanted, she left."

What he said was dubious, to be sure. When it came to Miss Mary Mullens, Caroline would not put anything past the woman. Such actions were not beneath her. It was difficult to think—why, oh why, had she drunk so much brandy!

"I tell you the truth when I say that I was disgusted by being forced to kiss her, for it was not something I wanted to do. Nor do I ever want to do it again."

When she turned and gazed into his blue eyes, she could see the truth behind them. "I believe you," she said, surprising herself. "If she ever threatens you again, you must tell me. Why Neil would take up with someone such as she, I will never understand."

"Caroline," Philip whispered as he brushed away a stray tear from her cheek, "I told you that one day I would be ready to move on from my past. That day is soon approaching. Please, be patient with me, and I promise that, as soon as my heart is ready, I will let you know."

She went to speak, but then his lips were on hers, his arms holding her close. This was a kiss she had never experienced in her life, for Reginald had never shown her such passion, a passion that reflected her own. When the kiss ended, she was left breathless, and she realized that she truly cared for this man.

"That was beautiful," she whispered.

His smile was full of love as he gazed down at her. "It was," he replied. "When this is all over, I will tell you everything, I promise."

"When what is over?" she asked as she slipped her arm through his and they headed back inside.

Chapter Thirteen

Caroline was struggling to keep her attention focused on the discussion of business she was having at the moment with Philip; her thoughts kept returning to the kiss they had shared the previous week. Her imagination was persistent in sending her mind to that day when she would be able to share how much she cared for him and to hear the same returned by him.

Although a small lingering doubt played at the back of her mind that Miss Mullens would cause problems, Caroline could not help but allow her heart to guide her steps. And her heart told her that he had indeed told the truth.

"Now, with your holdings in London," he was saying, bringing her back to the present, "you could divert a portion of the rents to a new property."

The scent of the man alone—a mixture of musk and orange added to that scent that was all his own—made it difficult for her to concentrate.

"I see," she replied in an attempt to hide that she had not been listening. "What do you believe I should do?"

Philip smiled. "It does not matter what I believe," he said with a touch of amusement. "What matters is whether you would like more holdings in London or if you would rather divert the funds to another city."

"Well," Caroline said, hoping to put her thoughts back to the meeting at hand, "London is the most beautiful city in the world, at least from what I have heard. Therefore, yes, I will advise Mr. Baxter to acquire more property as you suggested."

"Very good," Philip said, and Caroline hid her sigh of relief. Then he paused. "Perhaps you may want to go to London and see what is available for yourself. There is no reason you cannot do so, is there?"

Caroline had never considered going to London before—Reginald had gone on many occasions but always made excuses as to why she should not go—though she understood that most women in her position spent a vast amount of the year there. "As a matter of fact, there is not," she replied with a grin. "I must admit that, at times, I forget I am free to leave when I wish."

Philip gave her a smile. "You are, Duchess," he said as he placed his hand on hers.

Fire erupted in her stomach at his touch, and she slowed her breath to keep control. Would he kiss her again?

A scream resounded from outside, and the blood in her veins ran cold. She followed Philip outside where they came upon Miss Lindston, blood pouring from her nose and a bruise already forming on her cheek.

"What happened?" Philip demanded.

It took a moment for Miss Lindston to speak. "The...the boy..."

Fear coursed through Caroline unlike any she had ever known. "What of my son?" she shouted. "Where is he?"

The governess sobbed and her entire body trembled.

Philip placed a hand on her shoulder. "Where is Oliver?" he asked quietly.

"The river," she managed to say. "The men...they took him!"

Caroline heard screaming, and it took her a moment before she realized that those screams came from her.

"I tried to stop them!" Miss Lindston cried, burying her head in her hands and sobbing. "They beat me until I lost consciousness, and when I woke, I found this in my hand. I'm so sorry!" She produced a folded piece of paper, and Philip took it and read it.

"Take this," he said as he handed the paper to Caroline. "I will go and see if I can catch them before they get too far."

"Find my son!" Caroline cried out to Philip as he ran down the drive. She prayed Oliver would be found and returned to her unharmed, for without him, she had no reason to live.

***

Caroline sat with Miss Lindston as Margaret attended to her wounds. Miss Lindston continued to sob, and for good reason; her nose was likely broken and both eyes seemed to be blackening as Caroline watched. The woman was inconsolable, but Caroline was more than likely not the best person to do the consoling, for the anxiousness with which she suffered was close to becoming panic.

Philip entered the room, disheveled and with worry set in his features. "I am sorry," he said. "I could find no sign of them."

Caroline ran to him and buried her face in his chest. Now it was her turn to sob, and she held nothing back as he whispered consoling words to her. When she felt she could cry no more tears, she pulled away with reluctance and asked, "What do we do now? I read the letter…"

He held a finger to her lips. "Shh," he whispered. Then he turned to Margaret. "Will you give us some time alone?" he asked. "Speak no words of this to anyone. Let the servants know that if word of this is whispered outside the walls, they will be dismissed immediately."

With wide eyes, Margaret bobbed a curtsy and said, "Yes, Mr. Butler." Then she hurried out of the room.

Philip went to Miss Lindston and knelt before her. "I need you to tell me exactly what happened," he said in a soothing tone. "I know it was a shocking experience, but it is important for Oliver's sake that you leave out nothing."

"Yes, Mr. Butler, of course," she replied, wiping the tears from her face. She sniffed with effort, and Caroline handed her a kerchief. "Oliver and I had gone on our daily walk. He has insisted that we visit the place where he enjoys fishing since the day you and Her Grace took him there.

We were there no more than a few minutes when I heard the hoofbeats."

"Very good," Philip encouraged. "Now, tell me what you saw. Think very hard."

"There were five of them," the governess said, her brow creased in thought, as if that would force the memories to come forth, "and they had their faces covered with pieces of cloth with holes cut in them for the eyes. Four of them jumped from their horses and rushed at us. I pushed Oliver behind me and screamed that they could not do this, but they pushed me out of the way. I fell to the ground, and…and one of them began to kick me."

She was sobbing again, and Caroline put her hand on the woman's arm and gave her an encouraging smile.

It seemed to help, for Miss Lindston continued. "When they grabbed Oliver, I wanted to give chase, but I could barely move. Then one of them struck me so hard, everything went black." She gave Philip a beseeching look. "I swear, that is all I can remember."

"Thank you for your courage," Caroline said. She could have been the one who was attacked in such a brutal manner just as easily as this woman.

Philip nodded. "Please, go and rest. I must speak to the duchess alone."

The governess nodded and left the room, her sniffles heard as she made her way up to her room on the second floor.

Caroline fought the urge to run outside and scream. It was not easy, for she had to keep pushing away images of Oliver lying dead or hurt somewhere. "Philip, I am so lost as to what to do. What do you think? Who are these people?"

"They are clearly hired brigands. I worry that someone inside this home was somehow involved."

He must have noticed her alarm, for he quickly added, "We must assume the worst and hope for the best for Oliver."

"I will give them whatever they want," she said adamantly. "No matter if they request all my money and everything I own, I want my son returned safely to me."

"You will get him back," Philip said. "I promise you that. In most cases these people are after money." He began to pace. "When I went to where it happened, I was able to see that the story Miss Lindston told was true. There were five sets of tracks, though I do not know which one to follow to find Oliver. They were clever; they went off in five different directions, probably as a means to divert us finding him. What makes me worry is that harm may come to him if we do not find him soon."

Caroline nodded, pulled out the letter Miss Lindston had given her, and reread it.

> *We have your son. Tomorrow, you shall receive a second letter, which will contain a specified amount you must pay for his safe return as well as a place to bring the money. Do not alert anyone to the boy's absence or he will be killed.*

It was not signed.

Just an hour earlier, her world had seemed complete;, but in the blink of an eye, it had been turned on its head. An overwhelming sense of fear and guilt over what had happened to her son washed over her. She should have been with him. Perhaps then they would have taken her instead.

"I promised you that you and Oliver would never be hurt," Philip said, taking her into his arms once again. "I will not rest until he is returned."

Although she knew his words were true—that he would do everything he could—they did little to ease her heart, for although he could say the words, he truly could not promise that Oliver would be returned to her unharmed. That could only be guaranteed by those who held him.

***

The night passed with no news of Oliver, and as the sun rose, Caroline sipped at a cup of tea that had no flavor. She had not slept, and she was overcome with exhaustion, for her heart went out to her son. How she longed to have him in her arms again, to hold him and rain kisses down upon his cheeks. To let him know how great her love was for him. Caroline was never one to take her son for granted, not after Reginald had used him to hurt her. She had never considered anyone taking him from her in such a heinous manner.

Approaching footsteps had her turn, and Philip entered the room appearing as tired as she felt. "Today we shall receive the ransom note. It is important to remain calm throughout this process, even if your heart aches."

She set the now cold cup of tea on the table and nodded. Remain calm. She had been through horrific experiences in her life, but this was by far the worse she had ever endured. Her days spent locked away in her tiny room had been a blessing in comparison.

"I keep thinking Oliver should be waking soon," she whispered. "Do you think the people who have him will see he is fed? What if he cries for me?" It took everything in her to not begin weeping again, but she had to maintain some sort of calm lest she break down completely.

Philip placed a hand on hers. "You must hold faith that Oliver is strong and that he will need a strong mother to whom he will return."

She nodded, although the thought of faith seemed just out of reach. "You are right. I must do it for him." She reached into her pocket and produced a second letter, one she had written when sleep alluded her during the night. "I know it is silly, but I wrote a letter to the Duke of Ravens. Would you deliver it to him?"

Philip gave her a stunned look and then sighed. "I do not believe involving others is wise. Remember what the note said."

"Yes, I know. Perhaps the man will understand my pain and be willing to help. After what he endured with his own family..." She could not continue; the results of that situation had not ended well.

Philip took the letter from her. "Do not put faith in fables," he said, but he placed the letter in the inside pocket of his jacket anyway. "I will leave immediately to deliver your letter, but I must say that I do so with reluctance."

"Your reluctance is duly noted," she said with a small smile. "This is something I must do. If this man has any insight into how best to see my son returned, I will use it."

He gave her a bow and left.

She heard the front door close behind him, and Caroline walked to the window to gaze out over the garden. Her body screamed at her to sleep, but she knew it would never come, even if she went to lie down. Not until she received the promised second note. Then she could pay the vile people, and her son would be returned to her.

Chapter Fourteen

The hours crept by, and Caroline feared the ransom letter would never arrive. She had paced a rut in the sitting room floor and finally had gone to stand guard at the door, peering down the driveway for any sign of the letter that was promised.

Finally, a young boy mounted on what appeared to be a workhorse came riding up the drive. He had a friendly smile as he jumped from the animal to give her an unpracticed bow.

"You the duchess?" he asked, eying her skeptically.

"I am," she replied, trying to keep her demeanor calm. She did not want to scare this boy if he had what she had been waiting for. Yet, how he reminded her of Oliver!

"A man paid me a piece of silver to deliver this letter to you as fast as I could. I would've ran but that wouldn't've been very fast."

"And I appreciate your haste," she said. "Tell me, what did this man look like? Did you know him?"

The boy shrugged. "I don't know. He had a big stomach and an ugly face. Never saw him before and I don't know his name."

She took the letter he held out to her. "Thank you," she said. She placed a shilling in his hand, which he stared at with wide eyes. "For your hastiness."

He bowed to her again. "Thanks!" he said with a wide grin. Then he mounted his horse and rode away.

Her hands shook as she opened the letter. It had no seal, so it could have come from anyone. She read the contents aloud.

"In four days' time, you will deliver the sum of ten thousand pounds in exchange for the safe return of your son. You will go to a tavern called The Sharp Sickle in the village of St. Thomas. You will ask the landlord for a letter left for a Jane Covington. In that letter will be instructions for the exchange of the money for the boy. Come alone. Any attempts to alert the magistrates or anyone else will result in the death of your son. We have eyes and ears everywhere, even inside your home, so do nothing that will endanger your son. Trust no one, for you never know who is in our employ."

Fear went through her heart, and she looked up as Philip rode up to the front door. "Caroline?" he asked as he hurried to her.

Although the letter said to trust no one, she knew she could trust Philip.

She handed him the paper with trembling hands. "Here are their demands."

He read over the letter, and anger rose in his eyes, but he said nothing.

"And the duke?" she asked, hopeful. "Did he respond to my correspondence?"

"I am afraid he declined," Philip said with a sigh. "I was not allowed to enter, so the letter was given to him through his butler, who said that, although he understood your plight, he cannot come to your aid."

Caroline nodded, her head dizzy as though it was filled with cotton wool. It had been foolish to believe that she could put hope in some mythical duke. Besides Philip, she had little hope.

"Do not despair," Philip said. "We will go and retrieve Oliver. Do not give up; do not falter. The strength inside you is greater than you can imagine, and you must allow it to guide you."

His words awoke a small twinge of hope as he brushed a tear from her cheek. She was lucky to have this man in her life, even if he was no more than a friend. She had allowed her emotions to make more out of their relationship than what was there, but now she was thinking clearly.

Then a smile came to her lips as an unkindness of ravens flew overhead and came to rest in the branches of a nearby tree. She found it strange that a group of ravens was termed an unkindness, for the birds had their own form of beauty to them. Granted, their song had an eeriness to it, but it was ominous and lovely. Perhaps their visit was a sign that the duke would send aid after all, despite his initial refusal to help.

"You are right," she said, making no comment on the birds. "I do have a strength within me. But what if they see us coming? They said that I was to come alone."

"Worry not. You will pay the ransom and have Oliver returned to you. Although they are looking for a woman, a man they will see."

He started for the front door, but she laid a hand on his arm. "I do not understand."

"You will see," he replied. "Come. We must hurry, for we must leave at once."

***

Caroline looked at her reflection with dismay. How would anyone believe that beneath the shirt and waistcoat was a man? Neither piece of clothing did much to conceal the fact that she was a woman. The breeches were much more comfortable than skirts, and she wondered why women did not wear them more often. How much easier digging in the garden would have been dressed in breeches rather than that horrid dress!

She shoved the memory aside. It was in the past and had no place in the present. Nothing she could say or do would change the fact it had happened, so why spend her time remembering it?

A knock came to the door. "Come," she called out.

As expected, Philip entered. He looked her up and down and nodded approvingly.

"No one will believe I am a man," Caroline said with exasperation. "I am much too…womanly."

Philip laughed. "You would be surprised how many men have very feminine qualities," he said. "The coat will be concealing enough.

Now, put on the hat; that should help hide your face."

She donned the coat and hat, her hair already tied back so it could be hidden beneath. When she gazed into the mirror this time, she was pleasantly surprised at the final result.

"I would suggest not speaking if at all possible. Your voice could easily give you away."

She nodded. "I packed one extra set of clothing for myself as well as clean clothes for Oliver." Mentioning the boy's name made her chest constrict, and she had to regulate her breathing to calm her nerves.

She closed her eyes. *You have strength,* she thought. *Remember what Philip told you. You are strong and can get through this. Look how far you have come already.* For some reason she could not detail, she believed those thoughts. When she opened her eyes once again, a small sense of peace had returned.

"Excellent," Philip said. "I have provisions for us. And do you have the money?"

"I do." She went to a bench at the end of her bed and picked up a bag. It had not been easy procuring the large sum the kidnappers had requested.

"But, Your Grace," the man at the bank had argued, "carrying about that much money at one time can be risky. Why do you not allow me to write you a cheque for the amount you need, and I will see that it is covered when the receiver submits it."

Caroline pursed her lips in annoyance. "No, Mr. Redmark. I must have the funds in cash, or the man with whom I am doing business will back out of our agreement."

"What type of businessman deals only in cash?" the banker said with a click of his tongue. "I highly suggest that you be firm with this person. Or perhaps allow Mr. Baxter to…"

The force of Caroline standing made the chair scrape the floor. "If you cannot allow me to conduct business in the way I see fit, then perhaps I need to move my money to another bank."

The man's eyes had almost burst from his face. "No, no, Your Grace!" He had said in a shaky voice. "See that the duchess receives what she needs," he had ordered his clerk.

She had left the man close to apoplectic, though he kept his thoughts to himself after her threat, as she carried the bag of notes from the bank.

She chuckled at the memory. It had been the first time she had used her station to influence such an important man, and she could not help but have a sense of pride for that.

Holding up the bag, she responded to Philip's question, "I have the money here."

Philip gave her an appreciative nod before opening his coat and producing a large knife. He unsheathed it and held it up to her, the candlelight glinting off its surface. Placing two fingers on the front of her throat, he said, "This blade can pierce a man here," he moved his hands to her chest just above her left breast, "and here. Stabbing a man in the chest takes much more effort, as it is more difficult to penetrate the sternum." He returned the knife to its sheath. "Do not hesitate to use it if you believe at any time that you or Oliver are in danger."

"I do not believe it will come to that," Caroline said, or at least hoped, although the certainty behind the words was forced.

Philip leaned in toward her, his features fierce, causing her to take a step back. "You must not take time to think when it comes to either of your lives," he said, menacing. "You must act at once, or those lives will be lost. Is that clear?"

"Yes," she managed to say, although it escaped more as a squeak than a reply.

He sighed and shook his head. "I am sorry to have scared you," he said, his tone much smoother now but with clear effort, "but you must listen to what I tell you, for ahead of us lies dangers unlike you have ever seen. You have trusted me thus far, so I ask you to trust me just a little further. The question now is, do you?"

She did not hesitate as she nodded, although her heart had yet to return to its normal rhythm. He was right, of course; she did trust him. Would she kill to assure the safety of her son? Indeed. In a heartbeat and without thought.

He kissed her forehead, and as if he had heard her thoughts, he said, "Let us go and get your son."

***

Caroline was far from the most accomplished horsewoman, but Reginald had seen she learned to at least sit sidesaddle. Although she had learned, she was given few opportunities to practice; her outings had been restrictive, to say the least. If she had been taught to ride astride, the chances of her taking to it would have been much more probable.

Between the jarring movements of the horse and her tendency to grip the horse's flanks with her legs, it was not long before her back and legs began to ache. Notwithstanding, she made no complaint, for she would ride forever in order to save her son.

Roads gave way to small paths, which in turn led them through a dense forest. While it was eerie with its shadowy undergrowth and unseen skittering animals, for some odd reason, Caroline found its closeness comforting, much like a heavy, warm blanket during a thunderstorm. What did bother her was the beating she received from that closeness.

"Why do we not remain on the road?" she asked when another branch slapped against her arm.

Philip glanced back at her. "They may be monitoring the road, and it would be best if we were not seen before absolutely necessary."

His reasoning was logical. "And how long will it take us to reach St. Thomas?" she asked.

"Traveling through the forest as we are, we will arrive by tomorrow afternoon."

Caroline gasped. "Tomorrow? Will we find an inn in such a place as this?"

"We will sleep on the ground tonight," he replied with a chuckle. "I am afraid that you will not have the comforts of home on this journey."

"You forget," Caroline said with a sniff, "that I came from nothing; sleeping on the ground is not a new experience but rather one in which I no longer have to endure. My parents' cottage was a stone dwelling with a dirt floor, so do not presume I am so fragile I cannot endure one night sleeping in the open air."

She bristled when she heard Philip chuckle but then shook her head. What did he know of her past? Very little. So why would she expect him to understand her life before living in a grand house with more servants than she could ever use?

Once they reached the opposite side of the woods, they came to a steep embankment, Philip leading them down with practiced ease, which led to a small creek.

"We will stop to rest and water the horses," he said, sliding off his horse as if doing so was something he did often. Where had a gardener learned to ride so well?

Caroline could not help but laugh inwardly. She had made comments about him not knowing her past, and now here she was judging him for his.

She accepted the canteen he offered her and took a drink. The water was warm, but at least it was wet. "How do you know which trail to take?" she asked as she handed the canteen back to him.

He walked over to a large boulder and sat upon it. "Many nights I have spent in this forest," he replied, as if recalling a past memory. "And others like it."

"Why would you do that?" she asked. "Was there no work to be found?" What she meant to say was, what was a gardener doing traveling through forests, but that would have been much too intrusive to ask. He continued to be reluctant to speak of his past, and she had promised not to intrude.

He helped her back onto her horse and then mounted his before answering. "It is a story that is long, much like our journey. It would be much better told at another time." He clicked his tongue at the horse, and it moved forward. "Come. Let us ride while there is still light."

Caroline sighed as she kicked her horse and fell in beside Philip. The man had much to explain, but he was correct; now was not the time. One day, she would get him to tell her all of his secrets. And she found she could not wait for the telling.

Chapter Fifteen

The wood crackled as Caroline warmed her hands by the fire. She was surprised at how cool the night air was, and she pushed back the thoughts of her warm bed back at Blackwood Estates.

Philip sat across from her, staring at the flames. Although the man was typically quiet, tonight he was unusually so. He had said nothing as he set up the camp, and they had eaten in silence, even Caroline's attempts at making conversation rebuffed.

Yet, Caroline paid Philip little mind after a while, for her thoughts returned to Oliver and whether he was warm enough and had received enough food to eat. The poor boy had to be terrified out of his mind and missing her as much as she missed him.

She forced back tears and straightened her back. Soon she would find him and return the boy to where he belonged. Never again would she allow the boy out of her sight!

Caroline did not blame Miss Lindston. In fact, she admired the way the woman had fought in an attempt to keep Oliver safe. Her sobs and countless apologies had been met with genuine forgiveness, for if there was anywhere to lay blame, it would have been with Caroline herself. Philip had warned her that there were those who would work against her once they learned of the wealth with which she was charged, but she never imagined it would include the taking of her son.

Leaning forward, she rubbed her hands together for added warmth. Then a thought came to her that caused her to sit back. "How did they know Oliver would be at the river?"

"It may have been a moment of opportunity," he replied as he placed a piece of timber on the fire. "Perhaps it was unfortunate timing? Though I doubt that was the case."

"Do you still believe it is possible that someone inside my household informed them of his habits?"

He nodded without hesitation. "I see no other way. Word has traveled, no doubt, of the vast fortune your son has inherited and that you are the caretaker of that estate. These men were much too precise in their timing in taking Oliver. I believe they have done this before. In fact, I am sure of it."

"Then I must let all of the staff go upon our return," Caroline said with finality. "It pains me to do so, but I cannot trust anyone, it seems. I hate to see Margaret and Miss Lindston leave, but I cannot take any chances when it comes to the safety of my son."

"I doubt rather highly that either woman had a hand in this," Philip said. "My suspicions lie elsewhere."

Caroline raised her eyebrows. "Who would do such a thing?"

He studied her for a moment before replying. "I believe your brother-in-law might have had his hand in it."

"Neil?" Caroline said with a gasp. Then she studied the flames as she considered the prospect. "I suppose I can see it as possible. Yet, he is many things, but a kidnapper? No, he could not be that."

"Are you certain?"

She thought about it for a moment longer. The man had shown to have changed, and never had he mistreated Oliver in any way. Neil was a braggart and a fool, but he was not evil. Only an evil man could have done what these men had done.

"Yes, I'm certain," she replied. "He has his own money, to begin with, so there is no need for him to covet Oliver's. Furthermore, he loves his nephew, for that I have no doubt. Granted, his treatment of me had been as if I were a woman of lower class—which I was, I might add—from the first day I married Reginald. I have accepted his apology for his misguidedness, and he has proven to be rehabilitated.

No, there would be better ways for him to take Oliver's money."

"Like offering marriage to the boy's mother?"

The words made Caroline hesitate, and confusion moved through her mind. "I am afraid I do not understand. You approved of Neil being a part of Oliver's life. You insisted that I allow him to get close to Oliver and me." She narrowed her eyes at him. "Did you suspect he would do something this drastic? And if so, why would you put us in such a situation?"

"Taking the boy? No. His motives, yes. I have suspected them for some time now."

Caroline wrung her hands. How could this man have put her and Oliver in such a position if he had such suspicions? It was not that she doubted his honesty, but she found his words upsetting.

"Do not worry," he said as he stared at the fire before him, "I believe we will know who is responsible for this act soon enough."

She swiped at a tear that had escaped and rolled down her cheek. At the moment, bravery was the call of the day. "I am not worried," she said, although she knew it was not true. "I only wish to have Oliver returned to my arms where he belongs."

Taking a blanket from the pack beside her, she folded it to make a makeshift pillow and lay on the ground. The flames danced before her, mesmerizing. Her eyes refused to close, her worries were so great.

"The story you told me of the Duke of Ravens?" Philip asked.

She pushed herself up on an elbow. "Yes? What of it?"

"I know a story, as well," he said as he leaned against a large log on which he had been sitting. "Have you heard of the Duchess of Strength?"

"No," she replied, intrigued. "How old is the story?"

He reached for her hand and took it in his. "It does not matter how old the story is. What matters is the message it gives. Let me share it with you."

"I would like that."

"There was a woman who came from the poorest of homes. She married the richest of men, and soon rose to be a great duchess, and any who looked upon her were enchanted by her beauty.

Those who could hear her speak were amazed by the tenderness in her heart. Although life had not been what she had expected, she had a son who brought her great joy."

A hot tear rolled down her cheek. "Yes, he does," she whispered.

"The boy was taken, and with the aid of her gardener, the duchess rode for hours on end, enduring the blows of the limbs from the branches of trees in the woods and the harrows of steep mountain inclines. No ravens or other creatures led her; only the love for her only son guided her way. In the end, the duchess and the gardener found the boy, and the duchess and her son were reunited, never to be separated again."

"Thank you," Caroline whispered as her eyes grew heavy and sleep tugged at her. Philip had not released her hand, and she tightened her grip on him, willing him to not let go.

"Now, sleep," he said in a low voice. "Tomorrow's ride will be long, and what lays ahead of us will be even more taxing."

Caroline wanted to tell him how much his words had encouraged her, how much they had lifted her spirits. Sleep won its battle, and soon she was dreaming, knowing she was safe there beside him.

***

The hours crept by as they continued their journey. With each passing breath, Caroline knew she was getting closer to her son. The thought of having him in her arms again gave her the strength and courage to go on, even when she thought she might fall from the horse from exhaustion.

She had not slept well, her sleep filled with dreams of monsters wearing Neil's face chasing her through the forest in an attempt to kiss her. More than once she awoke with a cry, Philip beside her within seconds to sooth her once again.

They had been following the creek for several hours when they stopped to water the horses and rest. Philip broke off a hunk of bread and a bit of cheese and gave them to Caroline, which she took despite the fact that she had no interest in eating. Her stomach felt as if she had swallowed a stone, and the bread and cheese only intensified the sensation.

"You must eat," Philip said when she tried to return a large portion of the food to him. "You will need your strength to get through what must be done."

She sighed, knowing what he said was correct. With great reluctance, she finished off what remained of her midday meal and found that, somehow, she was able to keep it in her stomach.

Philip emptied the canteen and went to the creek to refill it. "We will reach St. Thomas by late afternoon and go straight to The Sharp Sickle," he said as he leaned over the flow of water. "There are a few things we must discuss beforehand."

"Very well," she said, taking the container from him and taking a drink of the cool liquid. It was much more pleasant than the tepid water it had held during their ride.

"Once you collect the envelope, I would like you to take notice if anyone is observing you. A young man stepping up to speak to the landlord should be of little notice, but if anyone is watching, they will take particular interest in anyone who approaches. I doubt that whoever is involved would not leave a lookout to see if you do as you were told."

"That seems a reasonable thought."

He nodded. "If you see anyone taking interest in you, I want you to do what you can to observe what they are wearing without being seen to do so. Do not openly stare but do what you can to study them. Then you will return to me and tell me what you saw."

"You mean you will not be accompanying me?" Caroline asked with horror as panic welled up in her. How could he even think that she would be able to do this on her own? "What if the kidnappers recognize me?" she stammered. "What if I am unable to be discrete and they follow me? What will I do then?"

He placed a hand on her arm. "You can do this. I will be waiting outside for you, but I want you to continue walking until you reach the end of the village where we will be stabling our horses. Do not worry; I will be right behind you. If anyone follows you out of the tavern, I will know."

"And what of the ransom?" she asked, forcing down her worry. She had trusted him thus far; she had to continue to do so or all would be lost.

"How do I know they will not take it and flee with Oliver once they have it?"

"At this point, you cannot know," he replied with a sigh. "We do not know what instructions they will give you next, but I will be watching for any trickery, I assure you."

She turned to him, lifted herself onto her toes, and kissed his cheek. "I doubt I will ever be able to pay you back for the help you have given me," she said as she lowered her feet back to the ground. "I am so far in your debt I do not believe it will be possible to repay you for all you have done."

He smiled down at her. "You cannot repay it," he said in a quiet voice, "for there is no debt owed. What we do is of such great importance, there is no price that can be placed on it."

His words gave her a sense of encouragement, and soon they were riding away, making their way closer to St. Thomas—and Oliver. She glanced up at the sky, glad to see that the weather had held. Only a few clouds lingered, just enough to cover the sun but not threatening rain.

For some time, they continued on until they found a road. It looked well-used, although it did not seem overly so. They came upon few people, and those they did encounter did not give her a second glance. Perhaps her disguise hid her better than she had thought.

Caroline wished to urge the horse forward to close the gap faster that lay between her and Oliver.

Philip counseled against it. "It would draw too many eyes," he had said, so she forced herself to maintain the steady pace. It pushed her patience to the limit, but she endured.

At last, they came over a rise, and Philip brought them to a stop. "Down there is St. Thomas," he said with a jut to his chin.

The village was small with perhaps fifty buildings in total. She could just make out the main street, which appeared to have no more than ten businesses. And just as Philip had said, stables had been positioned at the edge of the village on the side from which they would be entering. The remainder of the buildings appeared to be houses of varying affluence.

"The tavern is located in the village square. If you look closely, you can just make out the sickle used to hang the sign naming it."

Caroline squinted and scanned the buildings in the center of the village. Indeed, one of the buildings had a long tool that could very well have been a sickle holding a sign. How strange that this man was so well-acquainted with such a tiny village.

"From here, you will ride ahead of me and go straight to the stables. I will meet you under that tree behind the building—the one with the large branches touching the roof. Be sure not to speak to anyone unless absolutely necessary. We would not want anyone to realize you are not the man you seem."

Caroline closed her eyes and took a deep breath, tightening her hands on the reins. *I can do this!* she thought, and somehow she believed it, although she worried she would sick up at any moment. No, she *could* do this!

"I am ready," she said with firmness. She offered him a smile, clicked her tongue at the horse, and began the final trek of her journey.

Chapter Sixteen

As the horse trotted down the dirt road that led to the village, it took all of Caroline's willpower not to shout out Oliver's name. Was he in one of the nearby houses? Or perhaps one of the other buildings just beyond her view? If he was there, would he even hear her shouts? More than likely not, and if he could, he would not be able to respond.

She stopped the horse in front of the stables, and a boy rushed up to her expectantly. Without having Philip to help her dismount worried her, but she allowed herself to drop to the ground as she had seen him do and was surprised how easy it was to do so.

"Stabling him, Mister?" the boy asked as he took the reins.

"Yes," Caroline said, gruffing her voice to disguise it as she removed the carpet bag that held the notes for the ransom. "See he's given some oats, as well," she added before placing a copper coin in his hand.

The boy smiled broadly and pocketed the coin before leading the horse away.

Caroline heaved a sigh of relief. The men who had taken Oliver would not be as easy to trick. They would be on the lookout for her, so she kept her head low allowing the brim of the hat to shadow her features. Then she trudged up the dirt street, attempting to forget all of the lessons that Reginald had forced upon her, allowing her posture to sag and her steps to be less graceful.

It was not easy, but she did her best. No one seemed to give her a second glance, which eased her mind a bit.

Unlike Deptford, St. Thomas was a drab place with many buildings in dire need of paint and repair. Most of the windows had been boarded up or needed to be cleaned, and the few people she encountered lacked the joviality that she would have expected.

She made her way to The Silver Sickle and stopped to calm her racing heart. It would do no good to get this far only to faint before even entering the building from where raucous sounds emitted. The life of her son depended upon her keeping her wits about her. Taking a deep breath, she pulled open the door and entered the tavern.

What hit her as soon as she walked through the door was an unmistakable odor of stale ale and unwashed bodies, and her stomach flipped around inside her threatening to vomit her midday meal. She swallowed down the bile that rose in her throat.

It took a moment for her eyes to adjust to the dim lighting, and once they did, she looked around the room. It was dingy with soot-covered walls and tables that looked as if they had been broken more than once. Several men sat around the room, some alone while others had congregated in small groups.

She remembered what Philip had said and kept her head down while scanning the faces of those present. Most paid her no mind, of course. Why would they be interested in a random young man still covered in dust from his recent ride? Some of the patrons sat in shadowed corners, so she could not be certain if they took note of her entrance or not, let alone whether they cared about it.

Behind the long counter stood a large man with a bulbous nose and stubble on his chin as he dried a mug with his dirty apron. He spat in the glass, wiped it with the apron, and then set it with others on a shelf, making her feel ill. She might have grown up with next to nothing, but at least her parents saw that what they had was clean.

"Whatcha wanna drink?" the man asked as he rested his hands on the counter.

She cleared her throat. "I am here to collect a letter for Jane Covington," she said, remembering to add the gruffness to her voice.

The landlord snorted. "Sorry. Don't know what you're on about.

Besides, you don't look like no Jane to me."

Caroline was unsure what to do. She could not give away who she was, but what else could she do? She moved the hat back on her head and moved in closer so he could see her face. Then she lowered her voice, keeping out the gruffness this time. "I am Jane Covington," she said. "And I would like my letter."

His eyes went wide, and then he let out a boisterous laugh. "I get it now," he said. Then he reached under the counter and pulled out a folded piece of paper, which he placed on the counter in front of her. With trembling hands, she managed to open the letter only to find the paper blank. Was this some sort of game? Had Oliver already been taken away, or had the kidnappers changed their mind?

Then hot breath on her neck made her heart congeal. "Good disguise," a voice whispered in her ear. "Ye fooled me."

She went to turn, but he placed a hand on her shoulder.

"Not so quick," he said, the menacing tone in his voice making her shiver. "Ye got the money?"

"Yes," she replied, surprised at how calm she sounded. "Where is my son?"

"Close. Now, listen here. This is what yer gonna to do. In a moment, yer gonna head right through that back door."

Caroline glanced around until the door came into view.

"I left my horse waitin', and ye and me're gonna ride out to yer son. Don't look back at me or try'n call out fer help."

"I will obey," she said. "I just want my son."

He chuckled. "Smart woman. Now, get going."

She made her way to the back door, and she could sense the man behind her. No matter how hard she tried, she could not still her pounding heart, and she wondered how she could move on sluggish legs. They walked past a man who gave her a glance, and for a moment she hoped he would see the fear on her face. He walked past her without so much as a greeting, and her heart fell.

When they walked through the door, the sunlight blinded her, and she stopped and blinked.

He pushed her forward. "Get on with ye," he hissed.

She nodded and walked up to the only horse tied behind the building, a black stallion.

The man tossed a coin to young boy who was sitting on a barrel playing with a cat. "Ye ain't seen me, ye hear?"

The boy eyed the coin and gave the man a smirk. "No, Mister. I ain't seen nothing or no one."

Seeing the boy brought about thoughts of Oliver. "Is my son nearby?" Caroline asked and then nearly cried out as a hand grabbed the back of her neck and squeezed hard.

"Don't speak unless I tell ye to," the man growled. "Now, get up there!"

She managed to mount the horse, and the man pulled himself up behind her after he tied the bag of money behind the saddle.

"Right. It's time to go."

With a flick of the reins, he set the horse in motion. She glanced toward the tree where she was supposed to meet Philip, although she could not see it, and fear gripped her. Would he wonder where she was when she did not arrive as planned?

"Money and a duchess," the man said in her ear. "I think I'm gonna have some fun tonight."

Caroline could only force down the fear inside her and trust that Philip would find her. And soon.

***

As they made their way out of the village, Caroline no longer noticed the warmth of the day, or anything that was around them for that matter. Fear gripped her as they entered the forest. They were on the opposite side from where she had left Philip, and that scared her more than ever, for Philip would have no idea where she was.

Would he somehow learn that she had been taken? Yet, how would he have known? The landlord of The Silver Sickle knew she was a woman, but not he, nor any other man in the tavern, had taken notice of what had transpired between her and this man. Or they had ignored it.

In her heart, she knew her son would not be where they were going. This man meant to kill her and take the money. What would happen to Oliver?

That single question cleared her head. She could not count on Philip to find her, or Oliver, in time, so it was left up to her to keep her wits about her. If she was unable to escape the clutches of this man at this moment, she would keep her eyes open for the most opportune time to steal away. The man had to sleep, did he not?

"Ye sure are a pretty one," the man said in her ear. "And yer a duchess?"

Caroline raised her chin. She would not allow this miscreant to win. When it came to her son, she would fight with any means possible. "I am," she replied with as much regal air as she could muster. "And I have money, more money than you could ever imagine. If you see that my son and I are released without harm, I will see that you are given twice—no thrice—what I have in that bag."

The man snorted.

"Do you prefer jewels? Or works of art? Name it and you shall have it. Just let us go."

This caused the man to laugh. "This money'll do just fine," he said. Then he leaned in, his breath scorching her neck. "And maybe a kiss from you."

She could not stop herself from cringing, which only made the man laugh that much harder.

After some time, the horse came to a stop in a small clearing, and the man dismounted. Caroline looked around, but all she could make out were trees and grass in all directions. If she had not been taking note, she would not know in which direction she needed to go to return to the village. One thing was certain—no matter how loudly she screamed, no one would hear her.

The ruffian pulled her from the horse, and if he had not caught her by the waist, she would have been on the ground. That was not what she needed at this moment, a twisted or broken ankle. Any injury to her feet or legs would make escaping all the more difficult, and she was determined to get away to safety. Her life would not end in the hands of this scoundrel if she had anything to do with it.

"Now, let's see here," he drawled, yanking the hat off her head. He looked her up and down with an unsettling glint in his eye. "Yes, quite a lovely one ye are."

Caroline was finding every minute in this man's presence more and more difficult to stomach. She had to find a way to appeal to…. She almost laughed. This man would not have a good nature. Yet, she had to try regardless.

"Please, Mr. …"

"Ye can call me Pete. I ain't no mister nothing." The man snorted and then spat a large wad of phlegm into a nearby bush. No, the man was not anything close to being a mister anything.

"Very well, Pete," Caroline said, making every attempt to be appeasing. "I can see you are an…intelligent man. I am certain we can come to some sort of agreement. There does not have to be any reason for us to leave on bad terms. As I said before, I have plenty of…"

"And didn't ye hear me say that I don't care nothing for what ye have?" His eyes roamed over her again. "Well, maybe one thing…"

The air around Caroline seemed to dissipate, and she had to fight to keep herself from fainting. Fainting was not something she had ever done, nor would she allow herself to suffer it now. She had endured the wrath of Reginald for so many years; therefore, she could deal with this man without acting the weeping willow.

"Where is my son?" she asked.

"Far away, love," Pete replied. He ran a calloused finger down the side of her neck to the top of her left breast. "And truth be told, ye ain't gonna ever see him again."

Try as she might, Caroline could not keep the tears at bay, and they ran down her cheeks in easy rivers. She did not cry for herself, for she had lived a full life. No, she wept for the life of her son, for he was still so young. Oliver would never understand what it meant to be grown, to go on his first hunt, or to find his first love.

"Please," she said, now pleading. "There is no need to hurt me. There must be some shred of decency in you."

This made Pete guffaw as if what she said was of the greatest of humor. He patted the bag containing the ten thousand pounds and said, "Only decency there is, is cash, Yer Grace." Then he licked his lips.

"Now, before I kill ye..." He leaned in toward her, his lips puckered as if he meant to kiss her, and the panic set in. She would fight to the death to keep this man from ever laying a hand, or a lip, on her!

He was much too strong. He pulled her against him, but she fought him with a strength that came from her core. This man would not have her! She pushed, hit, kicked, bit, clawed, but the man only laughed and tried all the harder to place his lips upon hers.

As terror blanketed her, she lifted her knee into the man's groin. "Let go of me!" she screamed.

With a grunt, Pete released her as he bent over and grabbed between his legs. "I'll kill ye!" he grunted, the words coming with effort.

Caroline glanced around her in all directions. She had to get away! In the struggle, she was now turned around. The horse had moved away, as if to keep itself from harm as she and Pete had scuffled, and she no longer recognized from which direction they had come.

Oh, Philip! she thought, willing him to hear her cry. Then his words came to her.

This blade can pierce a man...

The knife he had given her before they left Blackwood Estates!

Reaching into the pocket of her coat, she retrieved the knife, removing it from its sheath, which she threw to the ground. Narrowing her eyes at the man and making every attempt to keep her voice from shaking, she raised the weapon at him and said, "I will ask you only once more; where is my son?"

Pete, still doubled over, smirked and then looked past her. "Been behind ye the whole time."

Without thinking, Caroline looked over her shoulder, soon realizing her error. She was a true fool for taking that bait. Before she could stop him, Pete grabbed her wrist, twisting it and making her drop the knife as if she were a small child caught with a stolen sweet.

"Now, yer really gonna pay," he snarled as he pushed her to the ground and began to remove his coat.

Chapter Seventeen

Philip knew something was wrong. Caroline should have made her way to the tree he had indicated by now, but he had not seen her as of yet. He cursed silently, debating with himself whether or not he should go out in search of her. He had no doubt he could trust her to follow his directions, but he also did not trust the men who had taken Oliver. It was clear they were scheming men, who would go to any lengths to get what they wanted. If it was not the money they wanted, what was their desire?

He clicked his tongue and urged the horse toward the main street, attempting to appear at ease. There was no sense in bringing attention to himself if she was in trouble. Unfortunately, he saw no sign of Caroline anywhere by the time he arrived at the tavern, and his concern rose.

A boy peeked from behind the building, and Philip called out to him. The boy's eyes went wide, and he slipped away. Philip cursed as he jumped from the horse and ran after the boy. It did not take long before he had the youngster in hand.

"Did you see a woman leave here? She would have been dressed in men's clothing."

The boy shook his head adamantly. "No, Mister, I ain't seen her." Something in his darting eyes told Philip he was lying.

Philip reached into his pocket and pulled out two silver pieces and held them up in the tips of his fingers. "Are you certain?"

Licking his lips, the boy eyed the coins.

"You know," Philip said as the boy seemed to weigh his options, "that lady is a mother looking for her son. Surely you would not bring harm to such a woman?"

This made the boy widen his eyes. "No, Mister, I sure wouldn't," he said. "She left with a man on a black horse; they headed that way, into the woods." He pointed off to the other end of the village.

"Good lad," Philip said, tossing the boy the coins. Then he reached in and took out another coin and threw it in the air. The boy caught it easily. "For making the right choice."

"Will she be all right, Mister?" the boy asked as he squinted up at Philip. "I didn't mean her no harm. The man told me not to tell anyone."

"She will be, so do not worry. You did not know."

With that, he urged his horse in the direction the boy had indicated. He had expected some sort of trickery, but now with Caroline and the money both gone, only one explanation could be made. They wanted her dead.

He came to a stop at the edge of the woods, searching for any clues as to which direction they would have gone once they entered the trees. One set of tracks led out of the village at that point; luck was on his side.

He glanced up at the sky. The sun was close to setting, thus the woods would be dim. He had a short amount of time to find her before something dreadful happened. Mounting his horse, Philip rode into the trees, keeping his eyes open for the continued signs of where the horse had gone. Few people used this track, so he read the way with ease.

At one point, he had lost the trail only to find it again past a rocky hill. He could only hope and pray that he was not following the wrong tracks, for if he was, the chances of him finding Caroline alive would dwindle to nothing.

After scouring the ground for the fourth time, he rose abruptly when he heard a woman scream.

Caroline! his mind shouted, the hair on the back of his neck rising.

He left the horse untethered and raced toward where he had heard the scream. He hoped the villain who had taken her had not joined his friends. Yet, if he had, then Philip would simply have to fight all the harder to get her free.

Scuffling sounds led him to a clearing where Caroline struggled with a large, unwashed man with matted hair and ragged clothing. No one else was about; luck was on Philip's side once again.

Where is her knife? he wondered. *She should at least…*

Then he saw it, on the ground as if tossed aside. It was as he thought; she had produced the knife but had it taken from her. What had he expected from a woman not accustomed to wielding a weapon? She was fortunate the man had not used it against her.

The man pushed Caroline to the ground and what he intended was clear. Philip could wait no longer; he had to pounce now!

And pounce he did. The man stared at Philip in surprise when Philip came racing from the forest edge and slammed into him with such force that the man went flying several feet before landing on his back.

Stunned, the man lay there for a moment, and Philip used this chance to free Caroline. "Go!" he shouted. "You must leave!"

Caroline screamed and Philip turned just in time to see the kidnapper barreling toward him. Philip grunted as the man's head plunged into his stomach. Breathing became difficult, and Philip lay stunned as he attempted to draw air into his lungs.

With effort, he forced himself to stand and caught sight of Caroline staring at him with wide eyes and her hand covering her mouth.

"Leave! Now!" he managed to croak once again and nodded with satisfaction when she did as he asked. Although anger still remained, he felt a sense of relief that she had escaped.

Lord grant her the path to return safely to the village, he thought.

Now that Caroline was safe, Philip glared at the man who stood opposite him with a ready stance. This man knew how to fight, but Philip had had his fair share of brawls in his life. As far as Philip was concerned, this man deserved what was coming.

"You dare hurt a Lady?" Philip growled. "You are nothing better than a beetle on the ground!"

Before Philip could react, the man hurled himself at Philip once more, but rather than feeling the pain of being winded, a pressure in his side caused him to stiffen, as if he had been cast in hot iron. Everything around him stood still; the leaves on the trees failed to flutter in the light breeze. The sun halted its descent. The air around him congealed, and Philip himself stood as a statue, his arms wrapped around his opponent.

Then, in the expanse of a breath, a piercing pain erupted in his side, a pain hotter and more excruciating than anything he had felt in his life.

"Now, you die," the brute hissed as he pushed Philip away, a malicious sneer on his lips.

Philip reached for his side and felt a wet stickiness. It was then that he noticed the knife he had given Caroline in the criminal's hand. When had he retrieved that?

The man cackled an evil laugh. "Ye think yer some great hero," he sneered. "But you ain't any better than any of us." Then he leaned in close to Philip's ear. "And that 'Lady'? I'm gonna make a lady out her all right."

He laughed again with such depravedness, Philip's stomach churned. In his mind's eye, he saw that which the man intended to do to Caroline, and anger rose inside him, a rage so great that Philip thought he would explode into a thousand pieces. Rather than shatter, Philip grasped that anger as a man grasping for a log while drowning. He pushed aside the pain and drew strength from deep within himself, and in one swift movement, brought his knee up into the man's chin, sending him reeling back. Philip heard a distinct *crack*, and the man groaned.

Philip picked up the knife the villain had dropped and stumbled over to where the man lay. Pressing the weapon to the culprit's throat, he said, "Where is the boy? Tell me now or you die."

The man shook his head. "If I tell ye, then you kill me."

"As my name is Philip Butler, I swear to you that you will live. Now, tell me where the boy is." He was finding breathing difficult, but he drew his attention away from his wound and focused on the man before him. "I have sworn on that name to allow you to live.

Speak! If you do not, you die anyway."

With a sigh, the man said, "He's being held in Chudleigh. You know the place?"

"I do," Philip growled. "How do I find him?"

"Outside of town, up in the hills to the east, there's a house. It's got an old tree that fell over in a storm. The boy's there. Now, are ye gonna let me go?"

"Who's responsible for this kidnapping?" Philip demanded.

The man closed his eyes and groaned. "I-I don't know. A friend came to me sayin' there was a job that needed doing. When I asked who was askin' to have the job done, he told me it wasn't any of my business, so I left it. But I was promised a lot of money for my part, so I didn't care none who was payin'. We took the boy and handed him over to a masked rider, and that's all I know."

"Who was the masked rider?"

"I'm tellin' ye, I don't know! I swear it! He never said nay a word to us, not even a grunt."

Philip nodded. The man told the truth. He glanced behind him to be sure Caroline had not returned on some whim, for no Lady should see what was about to transpire.

One thing that was certain was that letting the man leave would result in Oliver's death, a chance Philip could not take.

**

Stumbling down the indistinct path, Philip hoped his horse had not run off, the pain jolting through him with each step. The animal stood grazing on tufts of grass, looking up when Philip came toward him.

With much effort, he pulled himself into the saddle and made his way back to the village. Each step of the horse sent excruciating waves of pain, but he pushed them aside. Returning Oliver was too important to worry about a knife wound. He had bound it tightly with strips he had torn from his shirt and donned a fresh one to hide the evidence of his wound. Caroline would be frantic if she saw he was hurt.

Once in the village, he made his way to the tree; Caroline was an intelligent woman; she would know to meet him there.

He was pleased to see that he had been correct in his assumptions, for beneath the tree was Caroline, pacing. When he rode up to her, she gave him a relieved smile.

"Oh, Philip! I was so worried. I did not know who I should go to once I arrived, so I came to the tree hoping you would meet me here."

"You did well," he said, attempting to keep the pain from his voice. "Come, we must go."

She stared up at him. "Go where?"

"I will tell you once we are on our way."

Once she had mounted her horse, she rode up beside him.

Philip glanced at the sky. The sun had set some time ago, but he did not trust staying in the village. It would be too easy for those wishing to cause more trouble to find them.

She asked no more questions as they rode out of the village, for which he was glad. Besides the fact that anyone around could have overheard their plans, he also wished to keep hidden his wound. Women tended to fret over such things and they simply did not have time for that.

He stopped where a path led through a copse of trees. "We will camp in a clearing just beyond those trees for the night. There will be no fire tonight."

"I understand," Caroline replied.

They moved through the thick expanse of trees that would create a fine wall between them and the road. Few knew about this place, or so he hoped. They would need their rest to make it to Chudleigh before the sun set the following day.

When they reached the clearing—a space just wide enough to sleep only a handful of people—Philip eased himself from the saddle and dropped to the ground with a grunt.

"Philip," she said as she uncinched her saddle, "that man back there. What of him?"

He did not look at her as he unsaddled his own horse. "He will never bother you again," he replied. Caroline seemed to accept this without much thought, for she made no comment.

Once the horses had been rubbed down, they left them to graze in a small grassy spot. Caroline handed him a canteen. "I filled it before we left," she said.

"You did well," he replied and then thanked her before taking a drink. "We must rest now. We have a long ride ahead of us tomorrow, and I can't have you falling off your saddle from exhaustion. We should be fine here, but if you hear anything, anything at all, wake me."

She glanced around fearfully. "I will," she replied.

"Do not worry. We should be safe here."

With a final glance and a nod, she walked over and lowered herself to the ground beside where he sat leaning against a tree. Although he knew keeping watch would be in their best interest, the wound in his side would worsen if he did not rest. He closed his eyes and then smiled when she placed her head on his chest and took his hand in hers. He had little time to think of this comfort, for sleep overtook him almost immediately.

Chapter Eighteen

The following morning, Caroline followed Philip through the woods, keeping away from the roads once again. Worry plagued her, for her son, to be sure, but also for Philip. He had become quieter than normal, and when he did speak, his voice was weak and his face pale. She asked him three times if he was all right, but each time he assured her he was fine. Yet, inside her she knew something was very wrong.

The mid-afternoon sky held dark clouds that threatened rain, and she pulled the cloak she had packed in her bag tighter around her. She still wore the clothing of a man, but wisps of blond hair peeked out from under the hat, and she hoped no one would notice the curls.

"There is an inn an hour ahead of us," Philip said. "Tonight we rest there, and tomorrow, God willing, Oliver is returned to us."

"I pray you are right," Caroline said.

She glanced over at Philip once more. His hands gripping the reins were white around the knuckles and he sagged forward in the saddle. He was ill, very ill, but without him telling her what ailed him, she could do nothing to help. "Then the three of us will return to Blackwood Estates and resume our lives," she continued in an attempt to liven the sour mood around them. "Just because you saved my son does not mean you give up your position as my protector."

Her attempt at humor was met with weak laughter. "Serving you has been an honor. Whether you are a duchess or not, wealthy or poor, it has been a great privilege."

Her brows crunched at his words. "You speak as though you are not going to continue when we return. Such talk is foolish."

At one moment, the man was sitting in his saddle, and in the next he was sprawled on the ground.

"Philip!" she cried as she slid off her horse and rushed to his side. "Philip?" She brushed back his hair and was met with a face devoid of any color except dark bruises on his right cheek and blackness around his left eye. Yet, that was not enough to make a man fall from his saddle. "What is wrong? I demand you tell me right now!"

His eyes flickered, and when he replied, his words came out in an utter. "I was hurt. I did not want to slow our journey, for Oliver's sake."

Hurt? She could see no bruising beyond those that marred his face, so she opened his coat and gasped when she saw that the left side of his shirt was drenched in blood. She gingerly touched his side, and his eyes flew open as he let out a deep grunt. "I'm sorry," she said, "but I must see if there is anything I can do." He said nothing more as she unbuttoned his shirt and opened it to see a large, gaping wound. She touched it again, attempting to be more careful this time. Then her eyes went wide. The wound felt as if it were on fire!

"Caroline," he whispered, "you must leave me here. Go to your son. There is no shame in you leaving, for you must continue."

Tears welled up in her eyes, but she blinked them back. She had no time for tears. "No. I will not leave you here alone to die. Not after everything you have done for me." She began to remove his coat, which made him wince, but she had to get to the wound. "Now, I need you to summon your strength."

Philip nodded, and although he grunted when she lifted him to a sitting position, he did not try to stop her. She removed his coat and shirt, as well as what he had used as bandages before. From the canteen, she poured water onto a clean section of cloth and worked on cleaning the wound, flinching every time he flinched, pausing every time he groaned.

Once the wound was as clean as she could get it, she redressed it with fresh strips of cloth she tore from a petticoat she had in her bag and then helped him back into the coat.

"Thank you," he said, his voice so weak she worried he would pass out.

"Of course," she replied. "Now, I need you to summon all your strength, for you are much too heavy for me to lift."

He nodded again, placed his arm around her shoulders, and heaved himself, but once again fell to the ground with a groan.

"For me, Philip," she begged. "If you love me, stand."

Silence followed except for the songs of a few birds flying overhead, and she smiled when he put his arm around her shoulders once again.

"Good," she said, using all her strength to help him stand. Once he was up, his legs wobbled as she led him to his horse. "This will be more difficult, but I know you can do it."

He placed his foot in the stirrup and, with a grunt, heaved himself into the saddle with her help. Then she grabbed the reins of her horse and those of his and pulled herself into the saddle behind him.

"What are you doing?" he asked.

"I cannot have you falling again," she explained. "This way I can hold onto you and keep you safe." With a gentle flick of the reins, she set the animal in motion, her horse following behind them.

All her life, Caroline had dreamed of being happy, and she knew that Oliver and Philip had fulfilled that dream. There were those who sought to ruin what she had. Well, she would not allow them to hurt her any longer!

She had come from the poorest of families, someone who did not always have a full stomach or shoes on her feet. Then she had been raised to the level of duchess, a place in society of which one of her station could only dream. Yet, rather than joy, she had lived through years of abuse and deprivation.

Well, she had had enough of such a life! She was weary of the mistreatment from others. It was time for her to make her stand, to get back that which was hers! For she did have the strength to endure, and she would use that strength to complete her mission: to save her son, and to save Philip.

The birds continued their chorus of song, and one particular eerie tone made her look up to see the most peculiar sight loom above her.

Perhaps the emotions within, or the fear that threatened to overtake her, caused her to see what was not there. Regardless, what she saw was an unkindness of ravens circling overhead, as if guarding her and Philip as they moved forward in the direction of the inn.

***

The journey to Chudleigh was easier once they reached the road. No longer did Caroline have to worry about branches and undergrowth slapping at them as they moved through the woods, and she was able to urge the horses to a faster pace, which had them arriving in the village by late afternoon.

Caroline had secured a room, and with the help of one of the innkeeper's lackeys, she was able to get him into a large bed. At first, the innkeeper, a fellow as wide as he was tall with more chins than hair he had on his head, was hesitant to rent them a room. Caroline thrust a handful of notes at the man, which brought about a rather large smile and an eagerness to please that had been missing before.

She insisted that the man send for a doctor, who, as it turned out, was away and would not be returning until the following day at the earliest. In his place came an older woman, a healer as such, who wore a kerchief over her gray hair and carried a bag in one hand.

"Don't you worry," the woman said, a Mrs. Blither by name, "I mightn't be a doctor, but I know a bit 'bout healing. I'll see to your husband as best I can."

Caroline did not correct the woman. She had given the innkeeper Philip's surname, and he never questioned whether or not she and Philip were married, so she did not say anything to dissuade him of the notion. It also allowed her to ask for a shared room without any raised eyebrows.

Mrs. Blither pulled a wooden bowl from her bag and tossed in a handful of herbs and added a liquid of some sort, producing a revolting odor that made Caroline's stomach churn. Then the woman rubbed the mixture into the wound. "It smells bad," she said, wrinkling her nose, "but it'll do what needs to be done. His fever should break sometime tonight, I suspect.

The wound was deep, but the man holds strong."

"So, he will be all right?" Caroline asked, relief washing over her.

The old woman gave a grunt. "If he continues to rest, he will. I've done all I can do here."

"I thank you so much," Caroline said as she led the woman to the door. Then she reached into her pocket and pulled out a bank note, but the woman pushed it away.

"Mr. Comfry will take care of that," she said with a wide grin. "He told me how much you paid him." She huffed at this. "Downright dishonest of that man if you ask me. So, I'll see he uses some of his newfound wealth to pay me. But don't you worry none; I don't charge all too much." She let out a hefty laugh as she opened the door.

Caroline closed the door behind Mrs. Blither and returned to the bed. Reaching into a bowl on the nightstand, she rung out the washcloth and placed it on Philip's head. He made no reaction, which caused Caroline to worry all the more. He had not woken for some time, and she could not help but be concerned he would not wake again at all.

No, she chastised herself. *He will be all right.*

"You, my friend, are stubborn," she said, wiping at his forehead with the cloth. "We could have stopped and gotten help in St. Thomas, but not you! Oh, no, you had to keep moving forward. Now look at where that has gotten you."

She returned the rag to the bowl, rinsed it and wrung it out again. Then she placed it back on his forehead. "Just like how you risked bringing me water or telling those women I had taken a vow of silence." She shook her head and took a deep breath. "I will remain silent no longer." Good, her voice was firmer. "I love you, Philip Butler, so you had better not die on me."

Philip's lips moved, and her heart soared as she leaned in and heard him whisper, "And I love you."

Her breath caught in her throat. "Oh, Philip! You can never understand what those words mean to me. One day, we will marry, and you will help raise Oliver. The boy needs a father to teach him how to fish and how to be a man." Then her cheeks warmed. "And I need a husband, as well."

He made a small attempt at a smile, but soon he was breathing the soft breaths of sleep.

Once more, she rinsed the cloth and placed it back on his head. "There will be no more secrets, do you understand me?" She smiled knowing he had not heard her demand, but she continued to speak to him, telling him whatever came to mind. Of her life growing up in her parents' cottage and of her time working in the family garden. She did not speak of Reginald, for she had closed the book on that part of her life, never to have it opened again, but the rest of her past? He would know it all.

When she ran out of stories to tell, she yawned and looked down at the man she loved. "Tomorrow, I will go for Oliver, and this time, I will not hesitate with my fist or the knife. I am not a strong woman, not in the sense that a man shows strength in his muscles, but I am strong inside. You showed me this, and for that, I love you."

With another yawn, she removed her shoes and lay next to him on the bed, watching his chest rise and fall. Her eyes closed of their own accord as she waited for the sun to rise so she could set out and retrieve her son.

***

The doctor had arrived just as the sun began to rise. Caroline had been awake since well before then, having taken time to perform her morning ablutions and change into the dress she had packed. It was strange not having a petticoat to wear beneath it, but that had been torn apart to create makeshift bandages. She would have done it again if she had to.

Once the doctor had sutured the wound—Caroline had to turn away when he did this—he had produced a brown bottle and forced Philip to drink it. Then he stepped up to Caroline. "Mrs. Blither stabilized the wound, and the infection seems to have cleared a bit."

Caroline was relieved to hear this.

"He is not in the clear yet. The fever has not broken, which tells me that his body is still fighting off the infection. The next twenty-four hours will be of the utmost importance.

Once the fever breaks, I will have a better understanding of his prognosis, but it will take time, as will his healing after. Do not expect him to be up and running just because his fever has broken."

"Thank you," Caroline said.

The man chuckled. "Don't thank me yet, young lady. The wound was deep, but his body is fighting hard for him. It could go either way at this point."

"And how soon do you believe he will be ready to travel again?"

The doctor rubbed his chin. "As I said, it will depend on how long it takes for his fever to break. I would say that, if it is gone by tonight, he will need at least a week before he attempts to move. The chances of him breaking open that wound is great." He picked up his bag and walked to the door before stopping and turning back toward her. "Highwaymen set upon you and your husband you say?"

"Yes," Caroline replied. "We were able to fend them off and get away, but just barely."

The doctor nodded, but Caroline suspected he did not believe her story. At this point, she did not care; as long as he took care of Philip, that was all that mattered.

"Then I would suggest you keep yourself safe by staying here at the inn," the man said as he pulled the door handle. "He is not fit to travel, and you shouldn't be out there alone."

"I will be sure he stays here where he is safe," she said.

"Good," the doctor said with a smile. "Please send for me if he worsens. I will come by tomorrow to check on his progress."

Caroline closed the door behind the man and returned to her place by the bed. Philip's cheeks were rosy, as if he had been out in the cold for an extended amount of time, but he was breathing easier than he was when they arrived. She kissed his forehead and went to reach for the cloth from the basin when he grabbed her hand.

"Betrayal," he murmured. "It was Neil."

She stared down at the man in astonishment. "Are you certain?" she asked. Neil? Why would he do such a thing?

"Yes. I do not know…who the other is…but Reginald's brother…is one." His words came in short gasps, but they were clear. "Trust no one. Go home with Oliver."

"Philip?" Her heart raced when he did not respond, but when she placed her hand on his chest and felt him breathing, she relaxed. He had fallen back to sleep.

Frustrated, she wished he was well enough to explain why he suspected Neil. The thought of the man betraying her made her anger grow. She had to do something! They were much too close to where Oliver was being kept, and she could not wait another day to have her son returned to her.

She went downstairs and informed the innkeeper that she and her husband were not to be disturbed, except for the doctor or Mrs. Blithe, of course. Then she returned to the room and went straight for the wardrobe. Donning the shirt, coat, and breeches she had worn when they had left Blackwood Estates, she did not bother to look at her reflection before leaving the room and pulling the door closed behind her.

Once on her horse, she patted the front of her coat where she had hidden the knife once again. Whether the culprit was Neil or some other man, she would find Oliver and his kidnapper today. And whoever it was would pay dearly.

Chapter Nineteen

It did not take long for Caroline to ride to Chudleigh from the inn. She had urged the horse forward, paying little attention to those she passed on the road. Her mind was focused on one thing and one thing alone: recovering Oliver. The bag of money was tied to the saddle behind her and the knife was inside her coat pocket. Despite the fear that nipped at her, her anger was that much greater.

It was one thing to be denied seeing Oliver when she knew he was still in the house, and it was quite another to know he was being held captive by men the likes of Pete. If the other kidnappers were as baneful as that man, Oliver would be in grave danger.

Yet, what if Neil was the culprit in this kidnapping? Philip seemed certain that he had been the one to engineer this atrocity, and if that was so, he would learn soon enough what happened to anyone who threatened her as he had done. Gone was the meek wife of Reginald Hayward, and in her place was the true Duchess of Browning. She had given Neil something she had experienced few times in her life: mercy, twisting it and using it to his own advantage. Well, he would pay dearly for that mistake.

After some insistence on Caroline's part during the night they had slept in the clearing, Philip had shared with her what Pete had revealed about where Oliver was being kept. Now, ahead of her lay a split in the road, so she pulled the horse to a stop and considered her path.

According to the instructions that Pete had given Philip, she was to go to the right and the house would be located not far from here.

She patted the horse on the neck. "Please, guide me safely," she whispered and then clicked her tongue and kicked her heels to bring the animal to a trot again as they headed to the right. Soon, she came upon a house, but it lacked a fallen tree, so she moved on.

Just as she came to the top of a hill, troubled that she had yet to encounter the house and wondering if she had been misguided, she gazed down upon a small cottage in the middle of a large valley, no other houses nearby. Even from this distance, she could make out the large tree lying on the ground beside the house.

She had to stop herself from galloping onto the property and demanding the return of her son, for she had no idea how many men guarded him, nor how many weapons they might have. If she was shot in her attempt to save her son, the boy would die, as well, and she would not have that happen.

Instead, she approached slowly, and stopped just at the bottom of the hill, still some way away from the house. There, she tied the horse to a tree off the side of the road, removed the bag of money from the saddle, and began to sneak toward the house. She had never been very good at tracking, and the boots were much heavier than the slippers she was used to wearing, but she did what she could to make as little noise as possible.

When she reached the house, she took a moment to look around. No guards had been set and she could not see anyone looking out the single window at the front of the cottage, so she crouched down and ran to the side of the house to listen for any sign of Oliver being held there. She concentrated to hear anything, but no noise came from inside the house. With as much care as she could muster, she raised herself just enough to peek in through the window.

There, sitting on a chair, was Oliver.

Tears threatened to spill over her lashes as she returned to her squatting position. He was alive! Now, she had to somehow get to him without alerting the kidnappers.

Then a thought struck her, and she raised herself to peek in the window once again. The room was small and was a combination sitting room and kitchen with little furniture. How strange. What was missing was any other person besides Oliver.

She glanced around for any sign of anyone else, but not even horses whinnied in the rundown stables in the back. Had they left her son alone? Why would they do such a thing? Well, she would take advantage of their foolishness.

Remaining in a bent position, she ran under the window and up to the door. Once again, she listened but heard nothing. "Strength," she whispered as she pressed against the door. It creaked as it opened.

"Mother?" Oliver asked with wide eyes.

"Oh, Oliver!" Caroline cried as she ran toward her son. Before she could reach him, hands grabbed her and threw her against the wall, the wood scratching at her face. Then the hands let her go.

What she had expected to see when she turned was a ruffian, much like Pete, or even Neil. What she had not expected was the person who stood before her now.

"Miss Mullens?"

***

Anger coursed through Caroline like never before. The redheaded woman grinned as she took Caroline by the throat.

"So, you bested my man and found me?" she said with a sneer. "I knew his tongue was loose. I should have known better than to have entrusted him with such an important task." She glanced around. "Where's the money?"

Without thinking, Caroline reached for the knife in her coat pocket, but Miss Mullens was quicker and stronger, catching her by the wrist. "Now, now, you will not do that."

"Mother!" Oliver shouted as he ran toward them and kicked Miss Mullens in the leg.

The woman released Caroline, turned to Oliver, and struck him in the face, sending the boy flying to the floor.

Seizing the moment, Caroline grasped a handful of the woman's hair and gave it a good yank. "Oliver!" she screamed. "Run! Run out of here now!"

The boy stood, tears streaming down his face.

"Do as I say and go!"

Oliver did as he was told and ran through the open door and disappeared.

Caroline did not have time to do more than pray he was able to get away to safety. Miss Mullens brought up her fist, and pain shot through Caroline's jaw, making her legs go weak. Before she knew what had happened, she was on her back with Miss Mullens sitting on top of her.

"Why?" Caroline asked with a sob. "Why would you do this?"

The woman laughed. "You fool!" she said, her breathing heavy from her recent exertion. "A woman like you does not deserve the riches you inherited. I served your husband in so many ways; it should have been left to me!" She wrapped her hands around Caroline's throat and tightened her grip.

Caroline brought her hands up and grabbed Miss Mullens's wrists, but to no avail. "He was not your husband!" she managed to say as she continued to struggle to move the body that was on top of her. Although she knew the fight was futile—this woman had won in the end—Caroline prayed that Oliver would find help soon, but she did not have much faith it would happen. They were too far away from anyone else, and she had little fight left in her.

Tiny pinpoints of light twinkled in her vision, and images of Oliver being raised by someone else came to her. Would he remember her once he was grown? She hoped he would. Yet, who would be the one to raise him? Did anyone remain who she could trust? Would she even have a say in who that person might be?

No, she did not. She would die here in a cottage no bigger than the one in which she had been born. Besides Oliver, she would have no legacy, nothing left by which to be remembered. That thought saddened her even further.

Then again, she was not dead yet! Reaching deep down inside, she searched for that strength that Philip said would be there and she clutched at it, bringing a newfound sense of life to her. Raising her hips and twisting to the side, she threw Miss Mullens to the floor, but the woman flung a fist at her jaw.

Caroline saw stars in her vision as she landed on her backside.

"When I finish with you," Miss Mullens said through clenched teeth and narrowed eyes, "I will take Oliver with me. I will tell everyone that I am his mother and bleed his coffers dry!"

The woman's grin turned in to shock when a man yelled, "You most certainly will not!" Behind Miss Mullens stood a figure, his features darkened by the light coming through the doorway behind him. The man lifted an iron bar and slammed it across the head of the woman who had once been Reginald's mistress. Her eyes rolled back, and she fell to the side.

Panicked and confused, Caroline looked up at the outstretched hand. It was then she saw the face of the man who had saved her.

"Neil?" she whispered.

"Are you all right?" he asked.

She nodded and allowed him to help her stand. Her jaw ached and her sight had not fully righted itself, but at least she was still alive. She glanced down at the woman who had made her life miserable for so many years before following Neil out the door.

"Oliver!" Neil called out, and the boy peeked out from behind a nearby bush.

Caroline rushed to her son and enclosed him in a tight embrace and rained kisses down on his face until he grimaced. "Oh, Oliver!" She pushed him away and looked over him. "Are you all right? Did she hurt you?"

Oliver shook his head. "No. She was nice to me and fed me whatever I wanted. She even told me stories. I told her I missed you, but she said that she and Philip were my new parents now."

Caroline thought her heart had stopped. "Philip?" she asked. "That does not make sense."

"It will soon," Neil said as he let out a sigh. "I am afraid he has been behind this all along."

With weak legs, Caroline stood, her heart beating in her chest. "No! He has helped me this entire time. It was he who led me here."

Neil gave her a conciliatory look and then turned to Oliver. "Would you allow me to speak to your mother alone? Go wait over by that tree."

Oliver nodded and walked over to the nearby fallen tree, immediately climbing it.

"I must say, I am thankful that you saved me," Caroline said. Then a thought came to her and she took a step back. "You should be in France. How did you know where to find me?"

"I never made it to France," he explained. "I was besieged by highwaymen and held for ransom. Once it was paid, I was released, only to go to Blackwood Estates and learn that you had left…with him." He shook his head in amazement. "Although I thought it was only Mary behind this act, I began to suspect your gardener. Did you know he was caught looking through my ledgers?"

"I did," she said in a quiet tone as guilt washed over her.

He sighed. "On my journey here, I wondered why Mary informed me of his actions. That is, if they were working together, why would she tell me such a thing? Now I know she never meant to carry on with the man. It is clear she used him just as she had everyone else."

Caroline could not believe what she heard. Not her Philip. Not the man who had saved her, guided her, and most importantly, loved her.

Neil seemed to sense her thoughts, for he said, "He betrayed us all."

"I do not know what to believe," Caroline whispered.

He snorted. "You said he led you to where Oliver was being kept?"

Caroline nodded. "He did."

"Do you not find it odd that a simple gardener knew so much about this area?"

"I never thought…" Caroline could not stop her mind from reeling. From the beginning, Philip had been there, guiding her, instructing her. He knew information that a gardener should not know. Could it be true? Was he the man who had concocted this entire plot? "I will ask him," she said firmly.

"I suggest we leave for home immediately. You cannot trust that man."

"No," she said. "I must learn the truth."

She called Oliver over and embraced him once again. Her worst nightmare was over, for her son had returned to her arms. A new nightmare loomed before her, and it would be as horrible as the one she had just left behind.

Chapter Twenty

Returning to see Philip had been a difficult decision. She refused to let Oliver out of her sight, so he rode in the saddle in front of her where she could keep a precious hold on him. He was her responsibility, and nothing would keep the boy from her ever again. That promise she made with firmness as they made their journey through Chudleigh and off toward the inn where she had left Philip.

She felt nothing but bewilderment at what she had learned from Neil. Her heart was torn; who did she believe? Philip suspected Neil, and Neil accused Philip. Both could not be right, but who was the man telling her the truth? She had to weigh what she knew to make a decision.

Her first thoughts were of Philip. The man had been there when she needed him, when she was forced to work without food or water, when Neil had tried to take advantage of her. He had been the one at her side when she went to St. Thomas to retrieve the second note. And it was he who had rescued her from that vile man Pete, even receiving a horrible wound for his troubles. She did not wish to think about what Philip had done to that villain.

On the other hand, Neil had not been kind to her when Reginald was alive. Had he not explained his reasons? He had also asked forgiveness for his past actions, something she had never seen the man do. Furthermore, Neil had been taken himself.

How could he have been involved with Oliver's kidnapping if he was being held for ransom? And was it not Neil who had saved her when Miss Mullens had attacked her? Why would a man who was in league with the woman have done what he had done?

Her thoughts returned to Philip. He held so many secrets, and every time she pressed him about his past, he made promises that the day he could reveal all to him was closer. Had those promises been only a means in which to lead her astray so he could take her money and then leave with Miss Mullens? The last was the most uncomfortable, for that would have meant that he had taken up with the woman long before he had convinced Reginald to employ him.

By the time she reached the inn, her head was aching. So much stacked up against Philip. Was going to see him the best idea? She had to see him one last time, to see if she could get the truth from him, or she would wonder for the remainder of her life.

She left Oliver in the common room of the inn, a bowl of stew in front of him.

"You see he is still here when I return," she told the innkeeper with a stern glare.

The man wrung his apron. "He'll be in my personal care, Your Grace."

Satisfied the man would do his duty, she went upstairs and took a deep breath before opening the door to the room. A fresh bowl of water lay on the nightstand as well as a fresh washcloth. Mrs. Blither must have come by to check on him while Caroline was away, for the bed appeared to have fresh sheets. Caroline could not help but feel guilty; what had that woman thought when she arrived to find Caroline gone and her supposed husband left alone in his condition?

Well, what the healer thought should not matter to Caroline. The woman had no idea what she had been through in the past twenty-four hours, so who was she to judge?

Caroline laughed. She was defending herself when no one was about to cast judgment on her. Such thoughts were a waste of precious time, for Oliver had to be the most important person in her life at the moment.

She sat upon the edge of the bed and dipped the cloth in the water.

The fever still raged in Philip, and Caroline wondered if she should simply stay and care for him. If he was the culprit behind Oliver's kidnapping, did she truly wish to be in his presence?

As she placed the cool rag on his forehead, he groaned but did not awaken. "I found Oliver," she whispered as she dabbed at his face. "He is safe."

Philip did not respond in any way, so she continued to talk, hoping he would hear and let her know the truth.

"It was Miss Mullens."

With a moan, Philip moved his head but then went silent again.

"Neil saved us," she continued, hoping the news would incite more of a reaction. "He believes you were working with her all along." She rinsed the cloth, wrung out the excess water, and returned to bathing his face. "I saw you kiss her. Was I a fool to believe you, that it was for her silence as you said?"

Still no response.

"I do not wish to believe that you were involved, but I must admit that my confusion makes it difficult to believe otherwise. I love you, but I need to know why you have hidden so much from me."

A small moan escaped his lips, and she hoped he was waking. No words followed, and his eyes remained closed.

She gave a heavy sigh as she took his hand and kissed it. "I must return home with my son," she whispered, her heart heavy. "We will be traveling with Neil, for it is unsafe to stay a moment longer. I pray that when you are well, you will come to me and tell me everything." Leaning over, she placed a kiss on his lips. "I refuse to believe you would harm me or Oliver, but it is hard to look past that which I have seen with my own eyes. Goodbye, Philip."

"Betrayed you..."

Caroline's heart jumped into her throat, and she stood as still as a statue waiting for him to say more. Yet he did not.

"Who?" she asked, prompting him to continue; he lay silent, the only sign that he still lived the rhythmic rise and fall of his chest under the blanket. She hated to leave him here, alone and in his condition, but if he was the one behind Oliver's kidnapping, she had to get as far from him as she could.

The safest place for the two of them would be Blackwood Estates, at least according to Neil, and she could not agree with him more. There she had others who would protect her.

She stood and took one last look around the room. How strange that this had been the first place they had been as husband and wife, even though it was as a means to hide their identity. Her hopes had been that they would marry, but it was clear that was not meant to be. Glancing at the pile of clothing that was now folded on a chair, she noticed a letter that had fallen to the floor. Curious, she went over and retrieved it, noticing that the seal had not been broken.

Tears filled her eyes. She recognized that seal, for it was hers. It was the letter she had asked him to deliver to the Duke of Ravens.

Truly she was a fool for falling for his words. He had told her the duke had found her letter convincing but he could not help. Yet, the truth was it had never been delivered, a lie among many he had told her. Everything fell into place like a jigsaw puzzle, and the image on it was clear.

"Goodbye, Philip," she whispered, her heart breaking as she wondered how a man so kind could be in all reality so cruel underneath. "I wish to never see you again."

With that, she left the room, and the man she loved, forever.

***

Caroline had been in the carriage for several hours before she and Neil spoke of what had taken place. Oliver needed time to recover from the trauma he had endured, and speaking of it so soon would only intensify what had happened. Now, the boy lay asleep, his head resting on her lap.

Her son had been returned safely, and for that she was happy. The betrayal she had undergone with Philip had stung deep, and she knew it would take time for her to recover. Perhaps as long as it would take Oliver to recuperate.

"I had thought by allowing Mary into my home," Neil said with anger in his voice, "she could receive instruction and become a better person. What she did was not only unforgivable, but the shame I shall bear knowing it was happening around me makes me ill."

Caroline glanced over at his wrinkled face. "You were not aware of how far she would take her deception, Neil. Like you, I tried to do the right thing," she glanced down at her sleeping son, "and that decision was used against me."

He sighed. "You are right. Although, I will not forgive myself. To think they wanted to take Oliver as their own and raise him! The madness in the world is frightening." He shook his head and then gave her a smile. "But at least you are now safe, and that is all I wanted."

Caroline returned his smile. "Thank you once again for saving us from harm. I am in your debt, and I am sorry to have doubted you."

"Nonsense," he said with a snort. "My actions from before forced you to be cautious, and that was wise. You have a good heart, and I am sorry it was betrayed."

She gave him a nod. "Thank you."

He chuckled, but it lacked mirth. "We have both been betrayed. Now we have a bond I never would have thought we would share. I believe in the future we should take advice from one another. Would you not agree?"

"I believe that would be wise," she replied. Then she turned to look out the window. It would be dark soon, and they still had some distance to travel. Without warning, her thoughts turned to Philip, and she winced. Had his fever broken? Would someone be at his side when he woke? Or if he died? She shook her head. He had betrayed her; he deserved whatever was coming to him.

But death? Did he deserve to die?

She looked down at Oliver's sweet face and knew the answer immediately. If he was the guilty party, then yes, he deserved more than death.

Just having such a thought made Caroline sit back in her seat. Never had she wished death on someone. Even through years of abuse she never wished death on Reginald. Philip had betrayed her with her son, and that was not something she would accept. She had to harden her heart to him, for if she did not, he would return and break it again.

"When we return to Blackwood Estates," Neil was saying, "I shall send word to the magistrates to collect Philip. He will pay for what he did."

"I understand," Caroline said. Yet, it still tore at her heart. Did a chance still remain that he was innocent? Perhaps there had been some sort of misunderstanding. If not for the undelivered letter, she could believe so, but that letter spoke volumes.

"Know that I will never allow harm to come to you and Oliver again," Neil said as he placed a hand on her knee. "My life will be dedicated to protecting you both and making certain that one day Oliver becomes the duke he is meant to be. And I promise you, no one will stand in my way."

Smiling, she gave his hand a squeeze, and then he moved back into his seat.

"There is an inn not far from where we are. I suggest we stop for the night so you can get some sleep. It is unsafe to travel after dark."

She looked out at the setting sun and sighed. What she wanted was to be home where Oliver could be put to bed as he had before he had been taken. She wished for everything to return to normal in her life. What Neil said made sense; it was unfair of her to ask the driver to take them straight home and expect him to navigate the roads in the dark. Not to mention that the chances of highwaymen attacking a lone carriage in the night would be high.

"Very well," she agreed, "but I hope to leave first thing in the morning. Do you believe that can happen?"

He gave her a warm smile. "Of course," he replied. "For you, anything."

Chapter Twenty-One

It was a relief when the carriage turned into the drive the following day. Caroline had never been so happy to see Blackwood Estates in her life.

"Mother!" Oliver cried, "Our home!" He could barely contain his excitement, yet nor could she.

"Yes, my dear boy," she said with a laugh. "We are home at last." Home, where they could begin again, forget about the past and move on into the future she wanted. All her troubles were now gone, and only happiness would remain.

The carriage came to a stop, and Quinton opened the door with a bow to greet them. "Welcome home, Your Grace," he said.

"Thank you so much," Caroline told the butler as he helped her alight from the carriage. Once out, she closed her eyes and took a deep breath, exalting in the familiar smells of Blackwood Estate. "We are home," she whispered.

"That we are."

She had not heard Neil walk up behind her, and she turned to face him.

"I imagine you will be wanting to go to your room to rest."

Caroline nodded. "Yes. I must admit that, with all that has happened, I am fatigued." She turned to Quinton. "Would you see…"

A rider came down the drive, and Caroline could not stop the fear that gripped her. Would this be another man coming to kidnap her?

"Neil?" she asked in a choked voice when she saw the troubled look on his face.

"Oliver, go inside," Neil said without taking his eyes off the man on the horse.

Quinton took Oliver by the hand and led him inside, the boy glancing over his shoulder and giving his mother a fearful look.

"Who is he?" Caroline asked.

"A representative of the magistrates," Neil explained. "Allow me to do the speaking."

She nodded as the man came to a stop in front of them. He appeared to be of the same age as Neil. He dismounted with ease before walking up and grasping Neil's hand.

"Thompson," Neil said with surprising warmth, "we were not expecting a visit from you."

The man glanced at Caroline, his lip curled. "Her Grace is here? Rumors have it that some foul deeds have taken place. I must say, based on your appearance, I find them to be true already."

Caroline looked down at the coat and breeches she still wore. Her only dress had been left behind at the inn when she left Philip, that was how upset she had been.

She went to speak, but Neil interrupted her. "You will not speak to her in that manner," he said with a growl. "She deserves your highest respect."

The man snorted. "You old fool! Don't assume that you can speak to me that way. She's dressed as a man, an offense of its own." He turned to Caroline as he placed his gloves in the waistline of his breeches. "And from what I understand, you and your gardener have had some sort of romance while your child was spirited away. Is it true you allowed him to be put in harm's way?"

"I-my son was kidnapped," Caroline said, astonished that this man would put the blame on her. "It was my gardener who helped me find him."

"And where is this gardener now?"

"He is..." Caroline swallowed hard. What would this man think of her when she told him the truth? Yet, he had the power of the Crown behind him. "We left him behind at an inn in Chudleigh. He had been wounded.

He..." She turned to Neil and gave him a beseeching look.

"Thompson," Neil said in an appeasing tone, "please understand that she did run off with the gardener, but not in the sense that you suggest. She has done no wrong. I demand to know the meaning of this."

Mr. Thompson snorted. "By her own admission, she ran off with her gardener and put her son in danger. The man may have fooled her, but nonetheless, the boy was in danger by the choices she made. We will not allow that to happen again."

"Neil?" Caroline asked, her heart threatening to strangle her. "What does he mean?"

Neil waved his hand as if to silence her. "She has not had the benefit of the upbringing that those of us born into nobility has had. Surely you cannot mean to take away her son? I will not have it."

The man removed a roll of papers from inside his coat. "The proper documents will be presented to the courts, and within a week, the boy will be taken into our care. My hands are tied, Neil."

Tears streamed down Caroline's face. She never realized how much power the Crown had, but if they could remove a boy from his mother's care, they had great power indeed. She turned to Neil. "Please," she pleaded, "is there nothing you can do?"

"I will take full responsibility for the boy," Neil said suddenly. "If any harm comes to him, you may take my land, my money, whatever it is you deem adequate, but do not do this, I beg of you."

Mr. Thompson shook his head as if in thought. "I don't know," he murmured. "The boy cannot be left in the care of a mother who is willing to put his life in danger. The boy is to be a duke, but he is still too young to assume such responsibility. If she were married, her husband could take on the rights until the boy is of age, but to expect a woman to take on such responsibilities on her own..." The words hung in the air like heavy runs being aired on a line.

Caroline had to fight down panic. "Do I have no rights?" she asked.

The man laughed. "Women only have the rights granted to them by their husbands. Why do you think women are not allowed to own their own land? They haven't the mind for such things."

Her mind was clouded with fear, making thinking difficult.

Somehow, none of what this man said made any sense.

Before she could make any comment, the man said, "Expect myself or one of my associates to return within the week. Failure to produce the boy by then, or any attempt to hide him in any way, will result in swift punishment."

"Come," Neil said to Mr. Thompson. "Let us go inside and talk about this. I'm sure there is something we can do to prevent this from happening."

Mr. Thompson seemed to consider this and finally said, "Very well. I suppose you can treat me to a brandy while you're at it."

Neil nodded. "I suppose I can at that." When they entered the house, Quinton was waiting just inside the door to take the men's hats. "The butler will see you to the sitting room, Thompson. I will be in there shortly."

The man gave him a suspicious stare for a moment and then followed Quinton down the hall.

"What does he mean to do?" Caroline asked in a low tone. "How can they even consider taking Oliver from me?"

"I am unsure," he replied. "It seems that word has reached the magistrates that something has happened, but they are unsure as to what exactly transpired. I have seen this before, although it's rare."

"Seen what?"

"A child removed from a home where his or her safety is in question."

Caroline gasped. "So, they actually mean to take him away from me?"

Neil nodded. "That is exactly what he means. And because you are a woman, you have fewer rights than men. Come." He moved down the hall and she followed behind, though her legs felt as if they had been filled with iron.

They went to the sitting room, where Mr. Thompson sat in one of the high-backed chairs beside the empty fireplace.

Neil resumed his pacing. "What if she were to marry?" he asked.

Mr. Thompson narrowed his eyes. "I suppose if she were to marry, there would be nothing the magistrates could do."

"Marry? Why must I marry?"

He stopped his pacing and stared at her. "Did you not hear what the man said? If you had a husband who could keep you and Oliver safe, there would be no need to remove the boy from his home."

Everything had become a jumble in Caroline's mind. All she had wanted was to return home and take care of Oliver, but now even that seemed impossible.

Neil snapped his fingers. "I know! We can speak to Mr. Mullens. Perhaps he would be willing to marry you."

"Mr. Mullens?" Caroline asked with a gasp. "But, his sister..."

He gave her a sullen look. "I of all people know that a person cannot be held responsible for what his or her sibling does."

"Well, that is true, but..."

Neil began pacing once again. "No, Mr. Mullens is in France and not due to return for some time now. Even if I tried to contact him, we would not have enough time. With only a week, we find ourselves in a very difficult situation, to say the least."

She wanted to scream at him, to pummel him, to tell him that no one would take her son, but he continued his pacing and murmuring, suggesting one idea only to reject it a moment later.

Meanwhile, Mr. Thompson sat sipping at his brandy and saying nothing.

"But, Neil..." she tried once more.

Then he stopped, his eyes growing wide. "Why did I not think of this before?" he said enthusiastically. "Caroline, I want to ask you this only once. Do you wish to keep your son?"

"Of course," she replied, aghast.

"Then we shall save him." He pursed his lips and squinted. "You and I shall wed in a week's time." He turned to Mr. Thompson. "Will that bring this issue to a close?"

Mr. Thompson seemed to consider the idea. "You must understand that I will continue my investigation regardless. It would be a great benefit if Oliver had a male guardian." He set the now empty glass on a side table and stood. "I will return in one week to bear witness to your ceremony. If it does transpire, I would agree to the boy remaining in the custody of his mother and his male guardian. Have no doubt, if there is no union, the boy comes with me."

"We understand," Neil said, taking the man's hand and giving it a firm shake. "And thank you for giving us this opportunity to keep more disaster from this home."

Once Mr. Thompson left the room, Caroline sat on the edge of the sofa, the room spinning around her. What had just happened?

Neil returned from seeing Mr. Thompson to the door and walked up to stand beside Caroline, placing his hand on her shoulder. "There, now, it will all work out for the best. We have saved your son once again."

She nodded, although she could not find the words with which to reply. Magistrates, marriage, the threat of her son being taken from her once again, it was all more than she could bear, and she allowed Neil to hold her as she wept, his assurances that all would be well doing nothing to ease her fears.

***

With Oliver now in bed sound asleep and Neil on his way home with the promise to return the following day, Caroline sat on the sofa in the sitting room sipping a glass of wine. She had enjoyed a long bath, and although her body screamed to be abed, her mind was much too active to sleep. So much had transpired over the last week, and with the news today, everything had spun out of control.

Perhaps the representative of the magistrates, Mr. Thompson, was correct. She had failed to keep Oliver safe, and because of her inability to do so, he had been kidnapped. What if he had been killed? The thought of losing him in such a way tore at her heart, for she could not bear the idea of never seeing him again. Since that day when Miss Lindston had been beaten in order to take away Oliver, she had doubted her abilities as a mother. Mr. Thompson's proclamation only solidified those doubts.

She had never heard of children removed from their homes in such a way, but that did not mean it did not happen. There was much she did not know about the world, so she had to trust those who knew the law to help make decisions that would be best for her and her son.

The idea of marrying Neil made her skin crawl. Granted, she was more than thankful for what he had done to help save her and Oliver. If it had not been for him, she would be dead by the hands of Miss Mullens, and Oliver would have been whisked away, raised as the child of that woman and Philip. Her stomach churned simply thinking about it.

Also, if Neil had not been there when Mr. Thompson had arrived, she would have lost Oliver yet again. It was as if the world had turned against her, wishing her to no longer have her son in her life. Was it trying to tell her that she was not a capable mother? The idea frightened her, for he was the only important thing in her life. If she lost everything—their home, their wealth—she would still be happy as long as she had Oliver. And yet, was that fair to say that Oliver, in turn, would be as happy? He could never lose his title as long as he was alive, but would he be content living in a small cottage with a garden to fill his belly?

What would it be like to be married to Neil? He had assured her that he had changed, that he was not like his brother had been. Yet, could she trust him?

Could she not?

When she asked him about the time that would be necessary to prepare for the marriage ceremony, he had said it would be no issue.

"I will procure a vicar and prepare the necessary paperwork in time," he had said. "There are ways around the laws."

Despite her words, she faltered. The fact the man could do as he stated was not an issue; men in his position could move mountains, so that was not the reason. The fact of the matter was that she would once again marry for something other than love. Did she not deserve happiness after all she had endured?

A timid knock on the sitting room door brought her back to the present. Regardless of what she wished, she would go through with the wedding. She would endure this, and worse, if it meant that her son remained with her.

"Come!" she called as she took a seat on the sofa.

Her lady's maid entered and bobbed her a quick, but low, curtsy. "You wished to speak with me?"

"I did," Caroline replied. "Come in and close the door behind you. I wish to ask you a few questions, and we do not need any straining ears listening."

The woman did as she was told and returned to her place in front of Caroline.

"You worked for my husband for many years, did you not?" Caroline asked.

"Yes. Nearly fifteen years now. Before I was your lady's maid, I worked in the kitchen as an undercook."

"You know of what transpired over the past two weeks?" she asked. It was an absurd question, she knew, but it played into her plan. "With my son, that is?"

"Of course, Your Grace," Margaret said with wide eyes. Then she shook her head sadly. "Poor Miss Lindston was in tears about it. She still feels guilty. She's afraid to return; she's at her parents', she is."

"Yes, I am aware of her whereabouts. What I would like to know is what you can tell me about Philip Butler."

This made Margaret pause. "What do you mean?" The innocence the woman showed could not have been feigned. No, she had not been involved, Caroline was certain of it. The woman would know the staff intimately.

"When Mr. Butler first arrived, I saw him only a few times. What I would like to know was what you observed about the man. Where did he eat? With whom did he speak on a regular basis? Did he seem close to any one person over another?"

Margaret scrunched her brow as she looked to the floor between them. "Well, since the beginning, he was quiet, but he always kept busy. When others talked with one another—that is to say when they gossiped—he took no part in it." She paused for a moment and tilted her head. "Well, unless it was about Lord Hayward. I mean His Grace's brother." Her eyes shot up at Caroline, wide and fearful. "I don't mean to speak poorly of anyone, Your Grace!"

Caroline studied the woman for a moment. She was hiding something. "You have my word that anything you tell me is in the strictest of confidence. Not only that, but I promise not to be angry with you for whatever it is you tell me."

Margaret seemed to battle inside until she gave a firm nod. "See, when His Grace was...you know...unkind to you, I could feel anger rising in Mr. Butler. I..." Her cheeks reddened significantly. "I believe he cares for you. I've seen the looks he gives you, and those looks aren't for a servant typically has for his mistress."

Caroline stood and moved to the fireplace. What she wished to do was pace, but she could not be seen as agitated by one of the servants. That much she had learned from Reginald.

"I'm sorry if I've upset you," Margaret said, looking to the floor once again.

So, Caroline had not learned her lessons as well as she thought. Much the better, as far as she was concerned. A lofty mistress could take a deep fall if she put herself too high above those around her.

Caroline walked over and put a hand on Margaret's shoulder. "You have not upset me," she said with a smile. "There is no need to worry."

Margaret sighed with clear relief and Caroline returned her seat.

What was it about this man that had Caroline unable to create a clear thought? "I still care for him, though I should not," she whispered.

"Beg your pardon?" the maid asked, shock clear in her tone, though she tried to cover it.

Caroline laughed. Her words had not been for Margaret's ears, but now that they were out, she could not retrieve them. "Let me explain," she said. "But first, please, take a seat. My neck is cramping from looking up at you."

The poor maid was uncertain what to do, but she sat meekly in the chair across from Caroline, her hands wringing in her lap.

"You have been good to me during my time here," Caroline explained. When Margaret went to speak, more than likely in worry judging by the look on her face, Caroline stopped her. "I am going nowhere." This made the maid relax. "I have no one with whom I can confide, and you have been the closest to a friend I have had since I arrived. Therefore, I will tell what I have been through these past days."

Having a confidante brought a sense of relief as Caroline told Margaret everything, beginning with the journey to St. Thomas in search of Oliver to the secrecy Philip had maintained to leaving Chudleigh with Neil and finishing with the arrival of Mr. Thompson.

"So you see, my hand has been forced into marrying Neil this coming Saturday."

"Blimey!" Margaret breathed. "Oh, I'm sorry! It just came out."

Caroline laughed. "No, it is good to hear someone with an honest response that matches my own."

"But that's six days away," the maid said with a frown. "Quick if you ask me."

"If I do not do this, they will take my son away."

Margaret glanced around the room, as if in search of those listening ears, and upon finding none, she leaned in and whispered, "If you wish me to be honest, I don't believe Lord Hayward. Forgive me for saying so, for I know you're to marry him and all, but I've seen his ways. That woman, Miss French? No, you said her name was not French. Mullens. That's what you said. Anyway, I think the two of them are in league together if I had my guess."

"Did you see them speaking together at any time?" Caroline asked.

The woman shook her head. "No, nothing like that. It's just a feeling I have here." She tapped her chest. "And the way he looked at her was…immoral."

Caroline sighed heavily. "I must admit, I found it all odd myself." Then she remembered something the man had told her. "Though, Neil was held for ransom, as well. Then he stopped Miss Mullens from strangling me. Yet, deep inside, I find that I cannot stop believing that Philip was the honorable party in all this. Am I that much of a horrible person? Or am I too blinded by my own desires to see the truth?"

"No, Your Grace," Margaret said kindly. "Follow your heart. I'll say this, though. I know nothing of the *ton* or the laws of marriage—and forgive me for speaking poorly of those of your station—but it doesn't seem right they can just take away a woman's child. Not like that, at least."

Caroline shook her head. Although Margaret's words had eased her somewhat, some of what the woman said only added to the confusion. Neil appearing where she would never have expected. Philip not sending her letter to the Duke of Ravens. Miss Mullens's involvement. All of it sent her mind in a whirl. What she hoped was that the whirl was not part of a whirlpool in the middle of a vast ocean, for the chances of her not living through that were much too great.

Margaret patted Caroline's hand. "It will work itself out in the end, just you wait and see."

"I certainly hope so," Caroline replied.

Chapter Twenty-Two

Sunlight blinded Philip as he opened his eyes, the pain in his side that had run rampant before dulled to a low ache. His fever had broken the day before, and for the first time in some time he could think clearly. He struggled to sit up in bed when a voice came to him.

"You're awake!"

Philip turned to a portly man who he assumed to be the innkeeper due to the apron he wore. Had they met when he and Caroline arrived? If so, Philip had no recollection of it. As a matter of fact, there was little he remembered since the night that ruffian had stabbed him.

"That I am," Philip said, swinging his legs over the edge of the bed. He sat still for a moment, drinking in the pain that came with moving until it subsided enough for him to move once more. "Tell me, how many days since my friend left?"

"Friend?" the man asked. "Oh, your wife? She left three days gone now, My Lord." The man's voice was shaky, and he wrung his hands in front of him like a boy who stood before his mother when he was caught dipping a finger in the blueberry pie.

Philip glanced over at his clothes and saw the unopened letter. Had Caroline seen it? He truly hoped she had not.

"You-you're paid up and all if you're worried about that. Paid up 'til Sunday."

With a grunt, Philip said, "Thank you, but I will be leaving today.

Now, or at least once I am dressed." He pulled himself into a standing position. The pain was not as bad this time, but it still stalled him for several moments before he was able to walk to the chair where he began to don his clothing. It was a slow task; gingerly was the only course to take at the moment.

"Well...that is...I..."

Philip stopped with his foot halfway in a boot. "Out with it, Man. What is wrong with you? You seem a grouse who has realized a fox is on its tail."

"Well, My Lord, there is a problem. Now, I want you to know I had nothing to do with it."

Patience was wearing thin. "Speak!" Philip said, wincing as a shot of pain flashed through him.

The man glanced at the door. His fingers were turning white from the tightness of the apron strings around them. "It's just that there are some men from the watch here to see you."

"Men from the watch?" Philip asked. "And what have they said?"

"A woman was found murdered. They're inquiring about her with people in the area."

So, they have not found that man Pete's body, he thought. Then he chuckled inside. If they had, it was highly unlikely the watch would have been involved. Aloud, and with as much nonchalance as he could muster, he said, "And what has this to do with me?"

With a shifting of his feet, the innkeeper replied, "They been tellin' people to watch out for a man such as yourself—gravely injured in some way and actin' suspicious." Philip raised an eyebrow at him, and the man quickly added, "Not that I'm thinkin' you're actin' suspicious, of course, but they gave a description almost exact to you." He shrugged his shoulders. "Could be many men that've stayed at my inn, to be honest, but I thought I'd let you know regardless."

Philip nodded. "You have not told them I am here?"

The man shook his head. "No, My Lord. I...I don't trust 'em. There's not been any reason for me to think you'd be a murderer, and they didn't say nothing 'bout a woman being involved. Well, except the one who was murdered."

Philip would have laughed if the situation had not been so serious.

This man did not believe him to be a murderer, and yet he thought these men were searching for him. It made no sense. Then again, what reputation would an inn have if it harbored murderers? Perhaps the man was attempting to save face. "How many?" Philip asked as he stomped on the second boot.

"Two."

Philip reached into his pocket and produced two five-pound notes. "Fill a bag with provisions for three days," he said as he donned his coat. "Have it ready, as well as my horse."

The man stared at the notes. "But this is much more than I need in payment for that."

With a smile, Philip patted the man's shoulder. "Then let us say that the other note is for your friendship."

"But, My Lord," the innkeeper said nervously, "I don't think they mean you to leave."

Philip ignored him. "Have it ready," he repeated. "I'll be gone within the hour. Mark my words."

As he made his way through the inn, Philip rifled in his mind for a tale that would be worth telling. He had told many over the last few years, and he hoped he had one that would convince these men to see things his way.

Opening the front door of the inn, he was not surprised when two men stepped in front of him.

"Gentlemen," he said in a cordial tone, "I am pleased you are here. Please, let us talk, for there is much I would like to say."

***

Convincing the watchmen to see things his way had taken much more time, and a few more mugs of ale, than Philip had anticipated. His plan had been to be on the road by midday, but it was already well past three by the time the two men left the inn.

Pity I could not convince them to come with me, he thought as he threw the pack the innkeeper had given him on the back of his horse, tying it tightly with a rope. The man had been very generous, adding much more than Philip would need.

In all reality, it should take him a day to return to Blackwood Estates, but with evening creeping up on him, he could not risk a nighttime ride. He would be forced to sleep on the ground, and just the thought made his side ache.

Luckily, the innkeeper had also included a bottle of whiskey. If anything could dull the pain, that certainly would. Extra dressings and a small jar of the vile poultice from the healer had also been included. Philip would have to send a hefty thank you to both when all of this was over.

He was glad he had decided to take his time on his journey home, for no matter how hard he tried to grip his legs in an attempt to ride out the trotting of his horse, each jog sent pain throughout his body.

A bottle of some sort of brown liquid had also been placed in the bag, another gift from the healing woman, with a note stating that it was to help with the pain but also cautioning him from consuming too much. Apparently, it could force him to sleep, something he could not take the time to do. And if he was forced to sleep, then waking would be that much more difficult, and he could be easily set upon by brigands if he was unable to wake at even the loudest of sounds.

What his body needed was more time to heal, but he had to get to Caroline, to explain the truth to her, to explain why he had lied and about the things he had done. Only the thoughts of her kept him atop his horse, for each jolt of pain had him grasping the pommel of the saddle until the pain subsided.

When he stopped beside a small creek to bed down for the night, he removed the now soiled dressings, washed the wound with fresh water, and then poured a portion of the whiskey over the now clean lesion, making him clench his teeth to keep from crying out. Once it was redressed with fresh linen, the result was much more comfortable. Whether or not that would hold the following day, he did not know, but either way, he would not allow his injury to keep him away from Caroline.

The whiskey helped more than cleanse his wound. As sleep came to him—with a hope it would not be as heavy as the odious brown liquid—his dreams went to the woman who had stolen his heart.

Caroline waited for him, her arms open wide, ready to take him into her embrace. It was a relief to finally tell her the truth, to share about his past so he could become the man he was meant to be for her.

Yet, rather than accepting him, she pushed him away, angry that he lied. The love he had seen in her eyes dissipated, replaced by a hatred that made him take a step back.

"Why would you lie to me?" she demanded. "I learned the truth when I went to find Oliver."

"What truth?" he asked, confusion warring inside him. How could she have already known?"

"That it was you who had conspired with Miss Mullens to kidnap Oliver and take him from me!"

Philip shot up in an instant. Why had he dreamed such a thing? And then from deep inside his mind, he remembered her whispering this to him at the inn.

The sun cast a pink tint to the sky as it peeked over the horizon. It was time to be on his way, but he had to right the wrongs he had committed.

After redressing his wound, he mounted his horse once again. The ride was less painful this day, for which he was relieved; he was not sure he could have handled much more. Perhaps the poultice was some sort of miracle cure. Or maybe it was the whiskey—both inside and out—that had helped with his healing. Whatever it was that had helped him, he was thankful for it.

Several hours passed before he rode up to the massive stone pillars that flanked either side of the entrance leading to the large estate, and he urged his horse forward down the drive. In front of the house he came to a stop.

Although he had never been here before, he knew of its location; everyone who lived in the region did, for it was one of the larger, more impressive houses in the area. Four tall columns lined the front of the house, holding a triangular roof, reminiscent of the Greek ruins he had read about once.

A young stablehand ran out, and Philip tossed him the reins. "I will not be long, but he has had a long journey. Would you see he is rubbed down and awarded a bit of oats?"

"Yes, My Lord," the lackey said with a quick bow before rushing off to do what had been asked of him.

The door opened and a man stepped out, an odd smile on his face. "May I help you?" he asked as he watched the stablehand walk away with the horse. More than likely he wondered how a complete stranger would take it upon himself to order around a servant of someone such as he.

"Lord Franklin Mullens?" he asked.

The man narrowed his eyes; Philip had not offered him a bow. "I am he," he replied. "And who are you?"

"I am someone who is interested in certain business dealings of which you have been a part. Not only yours but those you have made with Lord Neil Blackwood."

The man sniffed. "My affairs are no concern of yours," he said in a harsh tone. "Now be off...Wait, I know you." He studied Philip for a moment before raising his eyebrows in surprise. "Are you not the Duchess of Browning's gardener?"

"I was," Philip replied. "I am now her protector, but that is irrelevant. I must speak to you; it is of the greatest importance." He glanced around. "Might we go inside?"

Lord Mullens raised a hand as if to keep Philip from entering. "I am sorry, but I have engagements this evening to which I must attend."

Philip made a step toward him. "Then I suggest you cancel, for I am here on behalf of the duchess herself, and it is imperative you assist me."

It took several moments for the man to study Philip before sighing and moving aside. "Very well. Come. We shall go to my office."

He followed the man inside and down a hall to a large room with little furnishings and bare walls. The only item of décor was a large globe on an iron stand and a bookshelf filled with what appeared to be books about various types of trade. Lord Mullens clearly had no interest in storytelling, which could be beneficial to Philip.

"Now, what is it that you need of me?" Lord Mullens asked as he handed Philip a glass of brandy.

"I would ask to look at some of your business ledgers." When the man went to argue, Philip added, "Trust me, it will be worth your time. Her Grace has left me with clear instructions, including several questions to which she would like the truth. Then you must take a journey with me, so I would recommend you see that your plans for the next few days are canceled." He held his breath as he waited the man's reply. If the baron refused and then asked Caroline to verify what Philip had said, all would be lost.

Lord Mullens gave him a shocked look. "I am afraid I do not understand. The duchess wishes that I cancel my engagements? And we are to travel together? To where, if I might ask."

Philip rose and stepped up to stand directly before Lord Mullens. "To the house of Ravencroft."

Chapter Twenty-Three

The dress that had been chosen for Caroline to wear was ivory with yellow ribbons woven around the sleeves and neckline as well as a yellow sash around her waist. A bath had been drawn, the water scented with lavender so even her hair smelled of it.

After toweling her hair dry, Margaret had brushed it until it shone and then painstakingly curled it using the curling iron, which was heated on top of a small metal bowl filled with hot coals. The preparation took hours, but Caroline wished to extend the time for eternity, for she could not stop the churning in her stomach.

By all accounts, she should have been happy, for in marrying Neil, her son would remain with her, and he would have a man to guide him where she would otherwise be unable. Yet, something still prickled the back of her mind, something that said that this was all a farce.

The problem was, to whom could she go to learn the truth? She had attempted to send a letter to Mr. Baxter, but it had gone unanswered. Perhaps he thought her a fool, the way most men saw women, and did not find the time needed to explain the ways of the law worthy of his time.

She walked to the window of Neil's office. He had insisted that they hold the wedding at his house, stating that to have her wed at Blackwood Estates would be in poor taste since that had been the home she and Reginald had shared together.

The idea that she and Reginald had shared anything made her want to laugh, but then she thought of Oliver. He had been the only good thing to come out of her marriage to the former Duke of Browning.

A raven landed upon the windowsill, and she gave a weak smile. It fluttered its wings and flew off, perhaps a sign that things were better than she thought. Then she sighed. She had trusted in such nonsense before, but now she knew no omens existed, for what had the ravens ever done for her?

No, she should not give up on what she believed, for if she did so, she would be left with nothing but the reality of the world around her, which was not as exciting or wonderful as the stories she had heard. Knowing the reason the Duke of Ravens had not come to her rescue was because Philip had not delivered the letter made her feel a bit better, restoring some of her faith in the tale that had kept her sane for so long.

Yet, she could not shake the feeling that something was amiss; although, she had nothing on which to place such suspicions beyond her own worries.

Sighing, she turned and looked at the bookcase full of ledgers. Philip had been caught by Miss Mullens searching through those books, a fact he had denied when she questioned him. But why? What did they contain that was so important that he would risk Neil finding out?

That something continued to tug at her. The answer to her problems was right in front of her, she could feel it, but it eluded her somehow. Thinking of Philip only brought about sadness to her heart, but it did nothing to ease the pain she felt. In fact, it only increased it that much more.

She hoped his fever had dissipated and that his wound was healing. Perhaps he would come to her and explain what had happened.

With a smile, she remembered their time at the beach and the kiss they had shared. Her cheeks burned; it was she who had initiated that kiss, and he had kindly pushed her away, telling her he was not yet ready.

A frown came to her face. They had spoken of being together, and although she had been the one to bring up such conversations, he had not denied it could happen. If they were to marry one day, which she had thought they would, then why would he wish to take Oliver for such a small sum in comparison to what he would gain if he married her?

None of it was comprehensible. He had seen all of her ledgers, had studied them, so he was aware of the wealth of which she controlled. What if she had been wrong all along? Perhaps…

The door opened and the fleeting thought disappeared before it could solidify in her consciousness.

"Caroline," Neil said with a wide grin as he entered the room, "the Vicar has arrived." He stopped and looked her up and down. "You look absolutely gorgeous, my dear." He leaned in and kissed her cheek. It was difficult not to cringe as he did so.

What a strange reaction, she thought. I am to once again marry a man whose kiss makes me cringe? Yet, this man was not Reginald. So much of what was happening to her left her head aching and her mind unsettled. Yet, her comfort did not matter; Oliver was all that was important now.

"Thank you," she replied. Then she glanced at the bookcase beside the desk and furrowed her brow. "Neil, why was Philip so interested in your ledgers?"

His smile turned into a frown. "Why does that matter now? We are to be married. What that man had been up to before has nothing to do with us now."

"I am simply interested to know," she said. "I find it hard to believe that he knew how I felt for him at that time. And then there is another question I have. He could have had access to my wealth, and yet he takes my son? Why would he do that?"

Neil sighed, taking her hands in his. "I do not know," he replied. "I have sent to have him captured, so maybe you can ask him yourself. Though I doubt he will tell you the truth now any more than he did before. Now, Mr. Thompson is here to witness the ceremony. Shall I tell him you are still interested in the man who initiated the kidnapping of your son? What do you believe he will think when he learns that you still have feelings for the man?

"No," Caroline said. "I am sorry. I did not mean anything by it."

She forced a smile. "Where is Oliver?"

"Miss Lindston is watching over him and will do so for the next few weeks." He pulled her closer to him, his eyes clouded with something she could not identify.

"What do you mean? He is not here for the wedding? I thought…"

"It was meant as a surprise, but I have no reason to keep it from you now. I have arranged a honeymoon for us." He smiled as if he had bestowed the greatest of gifts on her.

She was not as ecstatic as he seemed to be. She pulled away and stared at him aghast. "Honeymoon? But I thought this marriage was meant to be a farce, a way to save Oliver, not one that is genuine."

He chuckled. "My sweet Caroline," he said. "Surely you understand what marriage means. Must we live separated as you and Reginald did, existing in misery?"

"No, it is not that…"

Neil placed his fingers on her chin. "Then we shall have a happy marriage together, bringing up Oliver and his siblings in a home where they are loved."

That unknown emotion in his eyes grew as he spoke, and Caroline stifled a shiver at the thought of how those other siblings would come about. Her heart screamed no, but she nodded instead in agreement. And passing by the ledgers, she gave them one final glance, wondering what secrets they held.

***

The pathway that led from the back of the house was flanked by well-tended grass before it passed between a set of sculptured hedges until it reached a small covered shelter. Fear coursed through Caroline as she walked beside Neil toward where a man dressed in black clerical clothing stood.

Mr. Thompson waited to the side, a solemn look on his face. Thoughts ran through her mind as she remembered the cold man beside her who only months ago had wanted her in his bed in order to gain the wealth that was meant for her son.

It was those thoughts that had her once again doubting his intentions. Indeed, he had made changes in his life. Everyone deserved a second chance. She knew in her heart she did not wish to marry this man, and his words about having more children frightened her. One glance at Mr. Thompson told her she had no choice.

That man did not look her way, and an odd feeling of suspicion came over her. The man wore a smug smile, only making her suspicions grow.

"Neil, might I have a moment?" she asked, hoping being in the presence of the Vicar would pressure him into agreeing.

"But only a moment, my love," he said with what she recognized was an imitation of a smile.

She gave him a quick nod and walked over to Mr. Thompson. "I would ask you something, if I may?"

"Of course, Your Grace," he replied, though he pulled at the cravat at his neck as he answered.

"How long have you been in the employ of the magistrates?"

The man swallowed, his eyes shifting. "Ten years now," he said.

"Caroline," Neil said as he came to stand beside her, "is this necessary? We have a ceremony that must be completed. I am sure the Vicar has other business to which he must attend."

He gripped her arm, but she pulled away and rounded on him. What she saw in his eyes was clear. Greed. It had been concealed before, but now it shone as bright as the sun above them. Oh, what a fool she had been!

"We are not going to be wed," she said with a jut to her chin.

Neil leaned in, his face inches from hers. "Listen to me," he hissed, his eyes narrowing as he grabbed her arm once again, the grip so tight she cried out in pain. "You will wed me now. You do not deserve my brother's wealth. I do!" He pulled her before the Vicar. "Let us get this over with."

The Vicar gave him a dubious look. "My Lord, the Lady does not wish…"

"Do it now," Neil growled, "or I will have you removed from your position and cast out into the streets, along with her! And do not believe I cannot make it happen."

The Vicar nodded and began the words Caroline had heard before. She tried to pull away again, but the hold Neil had on her arm was much too tight. Tears ran down her face as the clergyman spoke the incantation that would see her married to yet another man she despised, and feared. And what would happen to Oliver once the ceremony was concluded? For he was the rightful heir to the Duke of Browning title and estate. She trembled. If Neil wanted it, he would see that an 'accident' took Oliver from her, she had no doubt.

As the ceremony continued, Neil shifted beside her. "Get on with it!" he shouted.

Then all went quiet as the sky above them darkened. Looking to the sky, Caroline's eyes went wide; hundreds of ravens flew above them, their cries deafening, their numbers such that they blocked the rays of the sun, creating a shadow on those in attendance.

With hot tears running down her cheeks, Caroline remembered the story her mother had told her years before while brushing her hair.

"And the Ravens knew of the duke's love for her, and so they guided him to where she was being held, leading the way and giving him strength so that neither would suffer ever again."

Neil glanced about, his face etched with fear. Then his eyes widened as he looked down the path. "Who is that?" he hissed.

Startled, Caroline pulled her arm from Neil's grasp and turned to where he indicated, shocked to see five men making their way down the path. One man walked with long strides before the rest, his dark hair flowing behind him. The birds above filled the nearby trees, their song bringing joy to her heart. For the first time, she understood the truth.

"It is the Duke of Ravens," she whispered.

Chapter Twenty-four

"What is the meaning of this!" Neil shouted as he grabbed Caroline by the arm and pulled her toward him. The words were filled with panic despite the mockery he made of his supposed position. Then his eyes widened. "You!" he said pointing at the man who stood in front. "No gardener will interrupt my wedding! How dare you!"

With some effort, Caroline withdrew her arm from his grasp and moved away from him.

"What? Do you not recognize me, Lord Hayward?" Philip asked with a cold smile.

"Of course I do, you imbecile," Neil sputtered. "You are that wretched gardener who kidnapped Oliver."

Philip pulled his head back and laughed. "You truly do not recognize me." He shook his head. "Interesting." As he circled the man, Neil turned, an animal trapped by that which had hunted it.

"You have no idea with whom you are dealing, gardener," Neil hissed, though his back was arched like a cat ready to attack. "This is madness, I will inform…." He then glanced at the other men who had accompanied Philip.

"Inform the watch?" Philip asked with an evil chuckle. "No need; they are here."

Two of the men stepped forward and each took hold of Neil's arms. "Unhand me, you fools!" he shouted, attempting to pull away without success. He stopped his struggles and glared at Philip.

"Who are you?"

With a sneer, Philip replied, "How is it that you do not recognize Philip Ravencroft, Duke of Greenwich? Surely you know the man whose wife and child you stole?" He towered over Neil, who shied away in fear. "Your days of kidnapping and murder are now over." Then he turned to Caroline. "Are you all right?"

Caroline looked up at the man she loved with all of her heart and replied, "I am." Then, movement in the corner of her eye made her turn her head. "That man," she said, pointing to Mr. Thompson who had inched his way toward the path leading back to the house. "He says he is a representative of the magistrates."

Mr. Thompson gave a small cry and turned to run only to be held by another man Caroline just now recognized.

"It was him!" Mr. Thompson shouted, pointing at Neil. "He paid me to say it! I didn't have nothing to do with any of it. He did it all, the kidnappings, the murders. He's been at it for years!"

"Quiet, you fool!" Neil said.

Lord Mullens tightened his grip on the man's arm, bringing about a string of words that would have made a sailor blush. The baron drew back his fist and struck Mr. Thompson in the jaw, which silenced the man immediately.

"Take his other arm, Grant," Lord Mullens asked of the fifth man, a man Caroline did not know, and Mr. Thompson sagged between the two men.

Philip walked over to Caroline. "Now, what did that man tell you?"

"He said he would take Oliver away. He claimed I am unfit as a mother and that if I did not marry, I would lose my son forever." Tears welled up in her eyes at the thought.

Lord Mullens walked up and bowed to Caroline, having left an unconscious Mr. Thompson in care of Mr. Grant. "Your Grace, rest assured that all of my business ledgers, as well as my testimony, will see that Lord Hayward is unable to bother you again."

Neil struggled against the arms that held him, but to no avail. "I will see you dead, Mullens," he hissed.

The baron snorted. "Perhaps the threatening of a baron can be added to his charges?" he asked the true magistrates.

Both men nodded, and one replied, "You can count on our testimony of his threat to kill you, My Lord." The smile the man turned on Neil was not friendly.

Caroline shivered, and the second magistrate turned to her. "There is no need for you to worry any further. He will not escape, I assure you. I have brought with me several armed guards." He glared down at Neil and added, "If he tries to escape, the guards have been commanded to kill him."

This caused Neil to stop fighting, and he paled as he lowered his head in defeat.

"Well, as exciting as all this has been," Lord Mullens said with a smile that would have been better suited for a ball, "I must be on my way. Rest assured that I will speak to both of you," he directed his attention to Caroline and Philip, "in the coming weeks. Oh, and before I forget. Your Grace, may I introduce His Grace, Philip Ravencroft, Duke of Greenwich." Then he turned, motioned to the Vicar, who had stared in aghast during the entire event, and they joined the remainder of the group at the entrance to the area, leaving Caroline and Philip alone.

"Oh, Philip!" Caroline cried as she threw herself into his arms. "You are alive—and here!" She pulled back when he winced. "I am sorry. Does it still pain you?"

He reached up and wiped a tear from her cheek. "I will heal soon enough," he replied. "And yes, I am here, my love, where I belong."

"You are the Duke of Ravens," she said in awe. "I do not understand, and yet, somehow, I believe I do." She wiped a tear from her eye. "That makes no sense whatsoever, yet none of this does."

Philip chuckled. "There is so much I must explain, and I promise I will."

"I would like that," she said, "for I have many questions."

He offered her his arm. "Then let us go inside, and I will tell you everything."

She put her hand on his arm. The others had already left, Neil and Mr. Thompson in tow. Caroline gave them little thought, for she could only set her attention on the man beside her. He had changed somehow. Not physically, for he still looked like the Philip she knew, but he stood straighter and held his head higher. Even his clothing was regal.

"Get us some tea," he said to the butler when they arrived in the office where Caroline had stood not an hour earlier.

The butler gave Philip a diffident bow and was soon gone, and Philip led Caroline to a sofa in front of the empty fireplace.

"Fourteen years ago," Neil began, "I was twenty years of age, naive, and married not a year to my love, Catherine. One day, I returned home to find her gone, a note left in her place demanding a large sum of money for her safe return. Like you, I attempted to pay the ransom; my only concern was to have my wife returned to me. When I arrived at the location where I was to collect her, I found her dead."

Caroline brought her hand to her breast. "Oh, Philip," she said, her heart breaking for him.

He patted her hand before continuing. "For years, I hunted down those responsible, finding them scattered throughout the land. None could have coordinated such an act, for they had not a single wit between them; therefore, I knew I had not found their leader. Then something Lord Mullens said one day turned my suspicions to one man."

"Neil," Caroline whispered.

"Yes. I overheard a servant speaking of your husband needing a gardener, and I knew it was my one chance to get close to his brother."

"Then, your reasons for coming to Blackwood Estates…"

Philip nodded. "Were to avenge the death of my wife…" He took a deep breath. "And my child."

Caroline gasped. "Your child?"

"Catherine was with child when she was killed."

"So, the stories were true," Caroline mused. "The Duke of Ravens had avenged the deaths of both his wife and child."

"They are true in that sense, yes," Philip replied.

"And Lord Mullens?" Caroline asked. "Was he involved somehow?"

Philip shook his head. "No. He was used, much like many others.

For many years, Neil has engaged in various illegal activities, and kidnapping and murder were only two; although, they were the worst. Apparently, he would find a way to earn money and then he would gamble it away only to repeat the cycle again and again. When he became indebted to a man who demanded payment in all sorts of sordid ways—I will spare you the details of such manners—Neil became desperate. That was when the kidnappings began. When he realized that holding people for ransom was such a lucrative business, it became his main source of income."

"Was Reginald involved?" Caroline asked, sickened by the idea that she would have been married to such a man.

"When I went through Reginald's ledgers, I noticed no issues, so I doubt he knew of his brother's exploits. It was when I searched the ledgers belonging to Neil that I found a notation for a large sum of money. He had invested into a business of which I had never heard, and this was immediately after I had paid the ransom, and for the same amount I paid. It was too much of a coincidence to ignore."

The door opened and Lord Mullens entered. "Ravencroft," he said, extending his hand to Philip." Then he bowed to Caroline. "Your Grace."

"Thank you for your help in this," Philip said, offering the man a chair.

As Lord Mullens took his seat, the butler came in with a tray laden with a teapot, several cups and saucers, and a plate of small cakes. "A gift from Mrs. Houston, the cook," he said with a bow.

"Thank you," Philip said.

Caroline studied the man who had once been her gardener but now she knew as the Duke of Ravens. He made himself at home in the house of the man who had murdered his wife. Perhaps it was a way of seeing justice done.

"I cannot express how sorry I am for all that has happened to you," Lord Mullens said as he accepted a cup of tea from Caroline. "My sister…"

"Oh, yes," Caroline said. "What had been her involvement in all of this?"

Lord Mullens looked at Philip. "Shall I explain, or would you prefer to do so?"

"By all means," Philip replied.

The baron sighed. "It appears that my sister was a mistress to Lord Hayward for some time before moving on to his brother—that is to say, your former husband. It is embarrassing to say, but when she learned of his gambling debts, she was the one to suggest the first kidnapping."

Caroline gasped. "How do you know this?"

The man grimaced. "When I learned she had been killed, I went to her home to retrieve her possessions, and I found her journal hidden beneath the mattress. It detailed every criminal act she and Lord Hayward had committed, including who else was involved and the amount of money they had gained." He gave a hollow chuckle. "She kept better books than even I do."

"I am sorry about your sister," Caroline said quietly. "It cannot be easy for you."

Lord Mullens studied her for a moment. "You are an incredible woman, Your Grace," he said finally, setting his teacup on the table.

She gave a light laugh. "How so?"

"Not many women would have tea with the brother of the woman who had been mistress to her husband and had played a part in the kidnapping of her son."

"What your sister did should not reflect upon you," she said with a smile. "That would be unfair to all of the good people in the world, for every family has one who, shall we say, does not conform to society?"

"Indeed," the man replied. "As it was, I also learned that Lord Hayward and my sister had planned to blackmail your husband, but he died before they could implement that plan. I believe that was what prompted them to take your son."

Caroline shook her head. "To have so much hatred, so much evil, inside had to be a heavy load to bear." As far as she was concerned, Neil and Miss Mullens had created their own burdens, and now both would pay dearly for their misdeeds. Miss Mullens already had, in all reality.

"Well, I must be off," Lord Mullens said as he stood. "Again, I apologize for everything you have been through."

"Thank you," Caroline replied.

He bowed once more, shook Philip's hand, and then left the room.

"Come," Philip said. "Let us go outside."

Arm in arm, they made their way to the garden once again, now alone. The sun shone on them, warm and comforting, yet Caroline could not help but feel sad.

"I was such a fool," she whispered.

Philip stopped and pulled her close. "You are no fool," he said in a low voice. "It has taken me years to unravel all this, but now, my heart is at peace and Catherine's death has been avenged.

"Will you be in trouble for the murders you committed?"

He shook his head. "Not at all. Let us just say that they were done in defense of my life, for when I confronted each man, he struck at me." When he saw the concern on her face, he added, "Truly, I killed those men, but I did so in retaliation for the lives of my wife and child."

"I am sorry for your loss," she said, wrapping her arms around him, gingerly so as not to add pressure to his wound.

He smiled down at her. "Thank you. She was a great woman, a woman of courage and strength...like you. I told you before that I was not ready for love, but for the first time in a very long time, I am. From the moment I first saw you, I loved you, and with each passing breath, that love grew. I am sorry I lied to you, but I hope you understand now why I had to do it."

Caroline nodded. "I do. I understand better than you realize. All of my life, I dreamed of falling in love and being happy. Oliver is my joy, and I have great happiness with him in my life, but you are my love. I never wish to be apart from you again."

"Then we will not allow that to happen." He leaned over and pulled her close, and when their lips met, Caroline felt a passion that matched her own. The feeling of a kiss that was given in love could never be matched, and the ravens perched in the branches around them seemed to caw their agreement.

Chapter Twenty-Five

The cool wind ruffled Oliver's hair as Caroline walked with him and Philip through the gardens of Blackwood Estates. Three months had passed since the day Philip had saved her from a forced marriage with Neil Hayward, and now, in one week's time, she would marry the man she loved instead.

It had been a whirlwind of events that had led to this moment, including a trial that had sentenced her former brother-in-law to be hanged a fortnight ago. Some women would have relished in being present for such an event, but she had chosen not to attend; she had endured enough as far as she was concerned. No sadness of his death resided inside her; although, regret that the man had such evil within him still lingered.

"So, next year I will be able to begin my horse-riding lessons?" Oliver asked as he looked up at Philip.

"That is correct," Philip replied. "Of course, I expect you to remain diligent in your studies. Although, I expect you will do just that, will you not?"

Oliver gave a firm nod. "I will, I promise."

They came to a stop beside a willow tree, its limbs swaying in the slight breeze. Caroline could not help but look upon her son and see the man he would become. Despite all he had been through—more than any one person would be expected to experience in their entire life—already he was thoughtful and caring and had a ready smile.

"When you marry Mother, will you still spend time with me?" The innocence of his question brought a warmth the sun could not have provided. The boy needed a strong man in his life; he craved such attention.

Philip squatted down, eye level with the boy. "Yes, I most certainly will. In fact, once your mother and I are married, we will spend even more time together. That is, if you would like that?"

Oliver did not reply with words but instead threw his arms around Philip's neck, clinging to him for several moments before pulling away. "May I go inside?" he asked, a twinkle in his eye. "I have planning to do."

Caroline had to keep herself from laughing.

Philip ruffled the boy's hair. "Of course you may," he replied, and Oliver ran off down the path that led back to the house. Philip turned to Caroline. "I believe the boy is far more excited than either of us for our wedding."

Caroline slipped her arms around him and smiled. "He adores you," she said. "And I can understand why, for I adore you, as well."

Philip smiled down at her, and she saw that emotion behind his eyes once again. Now, she recognized it for what it was. He cared for her as much as she did him.

They continued their stroll, and Caroline stopped in front of the large bed filled with flowers struggling to remain alive to spite the cold weather that had set in.

"What are you thinking, my love?" Philip asked.

"I was remembering digging through this soil with my bare hands, wondering how I would escape this life. Then you came into it, taking away that desire to leave."

"It took everything in me that day to restrain myself," he said as he placed an arm around her. "I could not bear to see you hurt. I believe that was the moment I fell in love with you."

"I adore how you gave me strength," she whispered. "You still do."

"I gave you nothing," he replied. "I only showed you that which you held inside already." Caroline went to speak, but he held up his hand. "That day I fell from my horse, my body was weak. I truly believed I could not go on.

And yet, a woman, strong in heart and mind, gave me her strength to stand and to go for help. Never doubt that you are strong, for you are the strongest woman I have ever met."

His words made her heart soar, and happiness spread through her body. "I will never doubt it again," she said. "Do not think me foolish, but although I know you are a duke, I cannot help but think of you as a gardener at times. It is how I remember you—a simple man."

Philip laughed. "Would you rather I return to my days of working here?" he asked with a wave of his hand about him.

"No," she said with a giggle. "I want you beside me forever."

He leaned in and kissed her, and that now-familiar flame inside her grew, threatening to consume her as the kiss became stronger and deeper.

She struggled to catch her breath when the kiss ended, and she placed her head on his chest, as if searching for support.

"We will be together forever," he said, his voice husky. "Whether duchess or gardener, it does not matter the title, for that which we share is most important of all."

As a raven came to rest on the branch of a nearby tree, Caroline knew in her heart his words were true. For she understood the meaning of strength, of courage, and of wisdom. They were used in the most dangerous and heartbreaking of situations, but all of them were guided by one thing.

Love.

Epilogue

A small cry woke Caroline, and she sat up in bed and strained to hear it again. Thunder rumbled outside and the cry repeated. She pulled on her dressing gown and made her way to the bedroom down the hall.

"There now," she whispered as she brushed back the hair from her daughter's forehead.

Thunder boomed again, and the girl pulled the blankets over her head.

"There is nothing to fear," Caroline consoled. "The storm brings rain, providing water for the animals to drink and the plants to grow strong."

Anne gave her a small smile. "So, the thunder helps, too?"

"Of course," Caroline replied. "Have you never heard the rushing of water from a waterfall?"

The girl nodded.

"Well, imagine how much noise a cloud must make to release the amount of water it does during a storm in the form of rain."

Anne thought about this for a moment and smiled again, this time much wider. "Mother, will you tell me a story?"

Caroline pulled the blanket to her daughter's chin with a nod. It had been five years since she and Philip had married, and they had begun a new life at Ravencroft Manor, leaving behind the dreadful memories of Blackwood Estates.

Philip still saw to the day-to-day workings of the house, for one day, when he was old enough, it would become Oliver's. It had been strange at first living in a new home, but Oliver had adapted quickly.

When Anne had arrived, he had been taken by his younger sister.

"I will protect you," he had whispered as he gazed into her bassinet, placing his finger in her tiny hand. "No one will ever hurt you."

Just thinking of that day made Caroline smile, and she leaned over and hugged her daughter. "Of course I will tell you a story," she said. "I will tell you a story my mother told me when I was young."

Her daughter yawned and wriggled down under the blankets, a habit she had whenever Caroline told her a story.

As Caroline began, she glanced at the door and saw Philip leaning against the doorframe, a wide grin on his face. He said nothing while Caroline told the tale, only moving to the bedside as she came to the end.

"And the ravens knew how much the duke cared for her, so they guided him to his love, leading the way and giving him strength. Since that day, neither of them suffered again." She reached over and kissed the forehead of her sleeping child, her heart near bursting.

Then, hand in hand, she and Philip stopped and peered into the bedroom belonging to Oliver. He had grown much over the years, but his sleeping form reminded her of when he was younger, so innocent and so angelic.

"You have done well," Philip whispered to her as she closed the door to the boy's room.

Caroline looked up at her husband and knew that her life had finally given her all that she desired. A man who cared for her, who gazed upon her with such love that she wondered how she had won the affection of such a wonderful man.

They returned to their own bedroom, and just as in the story she had told her daughter, she knew they would never suffer again.

Author's Note

I hope you enjoyed *The Duke of Ravens*. In the next book, *Duke of Storms*, Emma Barrington is willing do whatever it takes to save her father's business. Unfortunately, there are some men willing to take advantage of that fact.

Jennifer Monroe
Historical Romance with Heart

Jennifer Monroe lives part time in the state of New York and part time in Colorado and dedicates her time to her writing and her husband and two daughters.

She writes Regency romances with heart! With stories of first loves, second chances, dashing dukes, and ladies in distress, each turn of the page promises an adventure in love.

Not sure where to begin? Download her free ebook, *A Lady's Promise*, from her website – www.jennifermonroeromance.com – and have it delivered to your inbox today!

If you enjoy Regency Romances that center around siblings, you will love my nine-part series that begins with a marriage of convenience in *Whispers of Light*.

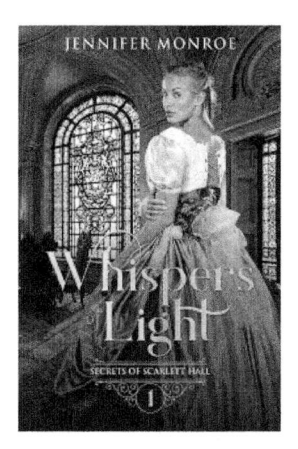

A Lady's Promise, the prequel to the Scarlett Hall series, tells of Miss Eleanor Parker's desire to wed the man she loves despite the wishes of an overbearing mother. Available for free from my website: www.jennifermonroeromance.com.

Printed in Great Britain
by Amazon